SHARDS *of* ICE

CATHERINE MEDE

FLYING KIWI PRESS

Dedication

To my Mums:
Mum, my biggest supporter, encourager, and beta reader.
Thank you for believing in me I love you Mum x x
My Step-mum, Beth – thank you for encouraging me to follow my dreams
Mother in Law, Sheri – thank you for your encouragement and the help with getting Cursed Love printed.

And my sister
Donna – the first person to buy one of my books. Love you

I'm so blessed to have these great people in my life.

PROLOGUE

The ground exploded in a shower of ice crystals where Vyvica Karala's foot had been seconds before. Vyvica somersaulted into the air, landing with a grunt on the cold, slick floor and rolling onto her side. Hastily, she took aim behind her, firing off her laser, but there was no returning fire.

The sniper had her pinned down.

Vyvica cursed as she huddled down, using a demolished section of wall as shelter. She crouched, listening. Claxons wailed around the entire complex, running footsteps were coming and going, laser fire bounced around the chambers.

Shouts of anger, surprise, triumph and terror filled corridors that echoed with barked out orders.

The command to retreat sounded in her ear receiver, but she couldn't. Not without her father.

Another laser blast hit the wall opposite her and she flinched. Taking a breath, she pressed her face against the cold surface, feeling its solidness underneath her cheek. Vyvica needed to get to her father's quarters.

If she could get him out, *then* she would leave the castle. But *only* if she could get him out.

Disaster had struck just an hour before; invaders hit the castle with such murderous force that the

D'Authian Guards were caught unawares. There hadn't been any news of a coup d'état, no hint of invasion. They were a peaceful planet. They had no enemies - that they knew of.

The city guards had scrambled to defend their posts, but timed explosions ripped open their lines of defence. She'd last seen her father in the throne room, declaring the order for retreat to be made, and the D'Authian Guards were told to leave the castle immediately.

"I must assist you to your vessel, Father," Vyvica had said.

"No, you're to follow orders, Karala."

"But what are you going to do? Wait here and negotiate?"

"If that is what I must do. You *have* to leave, Vyvica." He'd touched her face; tenderness softened his features before he pulled his mask of anger back into place.

"Follow your orders, Karala. What kind of soldier disobeys their superiors?" Her father's words rang in her ears. He'd had a point, but she wasn't leaving the castle without him. He had pushed her away then disappeared down this corridor. She had become caught up in the retreat until she found herself in the western wing.

Edging up to the top of the shattered wall, she glanced up and down the corridor, glimpsing a foot. For a sniper, he wasn't well concealed.

She ducked down behind the wall, positioned herself to face her would-be assassin and, using her legs, she launched herself over the wall. Skill kept her laser on target as she fired off a stream of plasma.

There was a grunt and a figure slumped on the floor. She ran towards his body and picked up his weapon. She leaned on the wall, peering around the corner.

The corridor appeared empty, but the sounds of fighting echoed off the ice walls and floors, rebounding around her in a cacophony of anger.

She ran with her heart pounding with fear, her breath puffing out of her as she hit the screen doors, throwing herself through them with as much force as she could muster. Her mind no longer focused on the castle invaders; her priority was to get her father.

"Retreat! Retreat! Retreat!" The words screamed through her ear receiver. She pulled the piece out and let it swing from its pin on her shoulder.

She cursed loudly but didn't hesitate, each foot pounding loudly in front of the other as she ran. Crashing through the last door, she met with a barrage of laser fire. Sliding down onto her knees, she attempted to fire back, but the blasts were coming from too many directions.

"Father!" she called out.

"Vyvica? For goodness sake, get out of here! Now!" His voice sounded muffled, and was followed by a bloodcurdling scream. It echoed from behind the door, freezing her heart with its agony. A strong arm locked around her waist, hauling her off the floor and back through the doorway.

"Vyvica? What are you doing? For goodness sake, girl, let's get out of here!" Someone pulled, dragging, and half-carrying her back the way she'd come.

"No, I have to get father!" She pummelled at her ally, unsure who carried her, her eyes blinded by unshed tears. Her mind reeled from the scream as she continued her frenzied attack.

"Vyvica, we have to retreat, did you not hear the order?" The arm around her waist let go, but grabbed her wrist and dragged her. She resisted, pulling against the strong grip. She recognised the colour of his skin and hair through the blur of tears; Tyron had her.

"Tyron, please!" she pleaded, tears dampening her cheeks.

"Vyvica, no. We have to go. You heard your father, he told you to leave. You can't save him."

You can't save him, ricocheted around her head. Her attention caught by those dreaded words. She planted her feet and pulled back, resisting the incessant tugging on her wrist. Her voice unnaturally calm and cold.

"I have to get my father." Using all her strength she pulled against Tyron, stopping him in his tracks. He spun and glared at her.

Tyron's stern voice addressed her. "Are you disobeying an order, D'Authian Karala?" Vyvica stopped listening. She continued to struggle, trying to get back down the corridor. "You have left me with no choice," he said. "This is for your own protection."

Vyvica didn't see his laser rise or feel it touch her arm, but she felt the charge before she blacked out...oblivion beckoned.

CHAPTER ONE

Five years later

"Alex, the simulants still need work, they only attack from the front. I need them to attack from behind." Vyvica barked into the comms unit on the wall.

"Yes, ma'am. Anything else?"

"Yes. They don't make sounds, very unreal."

"Right, ma'am. Apart from that, did it work to your expectations?" She detected sarcasm in the voice.

"No, and I don't appreciate your tone."

"Sorry, ma'am. I will work on the behind attack sequence."

"Do that."

"A 'thank you' would be nice."

"I beg your pardon?"

"Nothing, ma'am. Sorry, ma'am, didn't realise the comm was still on."

She contemplated pulling up the simulation again, but decided against it. The perspiration on her skin was already cooling. What she really needed was a shower to warm up before she caught a chill.

Wiping the sweat from her face, she pulled the tie from her black hair and let it fall in damp hanks down her back. She flicked a strand over her shoulder as she reached for her rehydration bottle and drained it, slaking her thirst as she contemplated the training room.

Windowless, the room had only the flickering overhead lights to keep it bright, like the rest of the warehouse and the underground city. Overhead lights provided the simulation of daylight and darklight. 12 hours daytime and 12 hours night time, every day. They set their clocks by it. The door whooshed open and Brett entered. He scanned the darkened room, but didn't appear to see her in the shadows. He turned to walk back out, but Vyvica moved with cat-like stealth and pressed her knife blade against his throat. He halted.

"Should've known you were there, Commander," he said, grinning widely.

"Should've looked better, Brett. Could've cut your head off."

"Could have, but you didn't. You like my face too much."

She flicked the knife, satisfied by his sharp intake of breath. She knew she had nicked him by the sharp metallic scent not far from her nose. She smiled.

"Enough of your lip, you need to show respect to your senior officers." His back straightened as he stared straight ahead, the smile gone from his face.

"Yes, 'ma'am."

"Can I trust you to think before you speak or act next time, or should I slit your throat now?"

"I will think, 'ma'am."

She hesitated. Brett was right, she did like his face, but she didn't suffer foolish behaviour either, and that could cost them if they ever had a combat situation.

She lowered the knife, prepared for anything, but fortunately Brett let the matter rest. Some of her senior men would turn around and attack her, to show their power, but each time she managed to leave them bleeding on the mat.

"What is the point of your visit, officer?"

Brett relaxed and turned toward her. His eyes flickered down, but returned to her face quickly. He knew better than to let them linger anywhere for too long.

She let him get away with it. She liked her lean body, and the appreciative glances from her crew confirmed she did something right.

"We haven't heard from Agnes yet."

Vyvica checked her watch communicator.

"Agnes was due to check in this morning, why are you only telling me this now?"

"Agnes sometimes gets delayed in relaying information through, but we have sent out someone to check." Brett swallowed hard. "Commander, it doesn't look good."

"What doesn't look good?" Her eyebrows drew down over her eyes as she studied him. This was the second network that she'd had trouble with in as many months. Usually information leaked out, but one network had already been shut down because they were too close to being captured. In a matter of minutes they'd been able to diffuse the group and get them to safety.

Brett fidgeted and his complexion paled.

Something was very wrong.

She pushed past him and marched down the corridor, her footsteps ringing out across the metal walkway. His footfalls hurrying behind hers sounded like he jogged to keep up.

Doors lined the walls, but some welded shut. A set of double doors came into view and they swept open soundlessly as she entered Command Central.

"What's going on?" she asked. Brett stumbled through the door behind her, taking his post at the Comms desk.

She returned the salutes of the officers in the room and eyed Tyron, her second in command. His furrowed brow, above his heavy dark his eyes, showed his stress.

"We sent a unit out to check up on Agnes, but this is all we found." He paused and sighed. "Prepare yourself, Commander." A video feed flickered onto the screen.

A horrific scene lay before her. All of Agnes' line was dead; shot, slaughtered, un-armed, with their hands bound behind their backs. Shot from the front.

Cowards, she thought.

Agnes lay on top of the rest, her body still. Vyvica shook her head, steeling her heart against the shock and pain.

"Is that her entire network?" she asked.

Ten bodies lay in the alley, lined up against the wall and shot, collapsing where they fell. The camera angle moved and zeroed in on the slain leader, Agnes. The livid bruises evidence of the beating she had taken before being murdered. Vyvica closed her eyes and heaved a sigh. Opening her eyes, her throat worked and her stomach lurched as she gazed at Agnes' ruined face. The death of an entire network, and worst, the death of her friend made her sick.

"Yes, from what we can identify." Tyron's voice interrupted her thoughts. Vyvica nodded.

"Do we know who did this?" Her eyes didn't waver from the screen as the video feed brought back images from the dimly lit alleyway.

Tyron shook his head. "No, 'ma'am, but we suspect who is behind it."

"Damn. How did they know who was in the line? No one knows except for the person above them."

"I can't say, Commander. But this looks like the work of Ch'ar."

"What makes you say that?"

The camera zeroed in on Agnes' arm, which lay out from her body. Her hand, closed into a fist, held a badge.

"That's convenient. Could be someone wanting us to think it was Barakus." She knew in her gut that nobody else held such a strong interest in their enterprise. "Damn," she repeated, stronger this time. She raked her fingers through her hair, hoping the action would fire her brain cells into providing the answer, but she knew that none would be forthcoming. "Enough. Cut the feed. We need to clean that up, give them a dignified burial."

"I'll arrange that, Commander." Tyron bowed to her stiffly as he pressed the button on the viewer. A pinprick of light in the centre of the screen provided the punctuation, the finality of the scene that she had witnessed.

Agnes was gone.

Holding her hands behind her back, she rocked on her feet, deep in thought. This war had taken its toll on the planet. She had seen enough killing and anger to last her a lifetime. She just wanted to reinstate the king on the throne and get back to her own life.

"I want a full report from the Unit when it gets back in." She turned on her heel and left the room. As the door slid shut behind her she could imagine the collective sigh at her departure.

Holding her back ramrod straight she marched down the corridor to her quarters. They had been lucky to find the abandoned warehouse in this section of the Underground City of Apos. The northern side of the warehouse was lined with rooms, three tiers of them. The bottom ones were officers, control rooms, interview rooms. The upper two levels, accessed via metal floored walkways protruding over the corridor, were used as sleeping quarters. It was originally meant to be temporary, but the situation at the Crown City of Althu had necessitated a longer stay.

Vyvica's footsteps rang out on the upper level of the walkway. Those leaving their rooms to start their shift moved aside, out of her way. She had been commander for three years and ran a tight ship. Agnes and Siara were her only friends; the only ones who understood her need to get back to her father. They were the ones that had got her back on her feet. Kicking and screaming of course.

And now Agnes...

Tightness gripped her heart, and coldness filled her gut like a hard stone. Her stomach roiled and threatened to toss her lunch back. Such a gentle soul as

Agnes did not deserve such treatment. Siara, now she was the opposite of kind hearted and gentle Agnes. Siara: tough, bitch, hardnosed. All good words to describe her. And that was why she and Vyvica got on so well. They could cut off their emotions and face reality without flinching. But seeing Agnes' battered body had taken all her strength not to show any reaction. Her steel face, as Siara would have called it.

There had been little love lost between Siara and Agnes, both claiming to be her best friend, yet she had found comfort with both of them. They each had values she needed and trusted. But her sense of loss with Agnes was strangely numbing. This kind of reaction from her own body surprised her.

She numbered the keypad to open her door and walked inside. Once the door shut, her shoulders sagged under the weight of responsibility for Agnes' death. She'd given Agnes charge of the network. Each person knew the name of the person underneath them. Not even Agnes knew everyone in her team.

Only Vyvica and Tyron did.

It shocked her to see Agnes' entire resistance network uncovered and eliminated. It would have taken them time to unfold the entire network. According to her records, they all lived in different regions of the Underground city.

Who could have done such a thing? The badge in Agnes' hand seemed too obvious, but she couldn't discount it.

The comms unit on the wall beeped. Checking her image in the reflective screen, there were no sign of tears or grieving. She breathed out before flicking it on, and Tyron's concerned face came up on the screen.

"Are you okay, Vyvica?" he asked quietly, exercising his right to call her by her given name. They had known each other for long enough, she could not demand he call her Commander.

"I'm fine, Tyron. Do you have news?"

"No. But I'm wondering if perhaps we need some outside help?"

"Why would we need outside help?" Anger flared, heating her face. Did he not think her capable?

"This isn't the first time we have lost part of a line, but it is the first time that we have lost an entire network. Vyvica, we need specialist help."

"You have something in mind?"

"Yes, someone. Kelvaras Mason."

"The vigilante? What would he be able to do?"

"Mason is more than a vigilante, Vyvica. He can infiltrate any network and find out where the leak is coming from."

"Do you think that is wise?"

"He's about our only hope right now."

Vyvica paused while she thought. She wasn't sure but, as Tyron said, they had little choice. They were only a small group with pockets of resistance networks across the planet. They weren't large enough to overpower Ch'ar and the republic. They couldn't afford to lose any more of their networks; that *would* be disastrous.

"I guess we will have to go with it." She sighed, rubbing her hands over her face. Tyron nodded.

"I will vid-com him directly. I'll let you know once we have received communication from him."

"Thank you, Tyron." Vyvica flicked off the screen, pleased that Tyron was second in command. She had to wonder what made the Council decide that she would make a good Leader. She hadn't asked to be the commander, and she didn't think she was capable of such responsibility. Every decision she made started with her, and ended with her, especially if it didn't go well.

Vyvica shivered. She'd been taught about her duty and her destiny since she was tiny. Recovering the Crown City was one thing. She would do it or die! But the rest? She sighed again. The weight of so much expectation was worse than the slim odds of success.

Fortunately nobody else, save Tyron, knew who she truly was, and she liked it that way. Not even Agnes and Siara. She wasn't out to make friends, just to do the job and get back to the castle and ensure that her father was fine. Only then could she fulfil her destiny.

Vyvica looked at her reflection in the screen once more. Her eyes looked tired, and her skin a little pinched, but she was all right. Straightening her back, Vyvica decided to focus on the future, and not think about what happened to Agnes.

She had to move on.

CHAPTER TWO

His travel pod was self-contained. It was, after all, Kelvaras Mason's home and it contained all his worldly possessions. He checked on the flight panel before flicking it over to autopilot.

"Autopilot engaged," a computerised female voice responded.

"Thank you, Vanya," he said, taking a last look at the panel before him. Satisfied, he headed to the back of the pod.

The pod, divided into three sections, held the cockpit, the living quarters and the motor. The motor hummed along nicely, had done since he had it reconditioned several months ago. Now she purred like a snow tiger.

Kelvaras headed to the bathroom in the living quarters. He checked his image in the reflector. He needed to create the right impression for his clients to take him seriously, and if he turned up scruffy and looking like he had been dragged backwards through the ice giant's patch he would be laughed out of town.

He was youngish, but determined. He knew what he wanted. Money. To get money, he had to work for it, and not all of it was above the law, but he didn't really care. He was often hired by law enforcement to help them with bounty hunting. They turned a blind eye to his more *illegal* activities as long as he accomplished his job. So far he had a ninety-nine percent success rate.

He didn't believe in a hundred per cent, that would be perfection, and he wasn't perfect.

He brushed his hair, washed his face, sprayed cologne around and checked his teeth. Although not vain, he had a reputation to uphold. As a solo operator he needed everything going for him.

Satisfied, he headed back to the cockpit. His vid-com flashed an incoming message. He flicked up the screen.

"Kelvaras Mason, this is Tyron Kwin." A pale brown face stared at him through the vid-com. "We have need of your services, would you please contact me immediately via return vid-com to discuss the situation and terms of agreement."

"Interesting," He knew the name Kwin, but the association with a group didn't come to mind.

His curiosity piqued, he touched the screen and requested a return message, initiating a 'search location' function on the comms, a special little feature he'd developed himself.

"Tyron Kwin."

"Tyron, this is Kelvaras Mason."

"Mr Mason. Thank you for answering me so promptly. We have an issue and we need your services. Are you able to help us out?"

"What services do you require?"

"We are a clandestine outfit. We require your utmost secrecy. If you don't want to, we will find someone else."

"Good luck with that," Kelvaras said, but he didn't move. He watched the older man's face in the vid screen. Tyron's eyes looked strained, a muscle in his neck bunched and released. A man looking for some answers, and Kelvaras would be able to help out.

"Yes, well it may come to that yet. What are your terms?"

"Ten mill up front, in cash. We can negotiate at the meeting what the rest of the terms will be, but I'm thinking that there needs to be a fairly good incentive for me to assist you-" He had a hunch, and took a punt. "Considering Ch'ar is looking for you."

Tyron sighed loudly, blowing out his cheeks. "We will give you what we can, but will only pay if you actually help. We aren't going to pay just for inviting you."

"That's fair." Kelvaras conceded. He nodded, happy he'd found out their little secret. Ch'ar would be very interested in that little titbit of information. "Where do you want me to meet up with you?"

"We aren't stupid." Anger flared in the man's voice, but Kelvaras was pleased to hear that they weren't going to tell him where they were. "We will meet you at the Port of Apos. Will tomorrow be enough time for you?"

"Mmmm. Tomorrow... I think that should be good. Afternoon? Early?"

"Two pm?"

"Done. See you there." Kelvaras flicked off the vid-com without waiting for a farewell. Port of Apos. That meant they could be in one of the four quadrants of the Underground City of Apos, or at least not far from it. It gave him a day to check out the Port and see what he could find out.

He pushed the "Find location" button, but nothing came up. He pressed the button again. Either the wiring was faulty, or they'd jammed the signal. He instinctively knew that the wiring was fine. He grinned as he thought about the meeting tomorrow. At least he had a starting point. They couldn't be far from there.

"Three minutes to entry of the Crown City Precinct," a computerised female voice interrupted his thoughts. "Would you like to take control?"

"Thank you, Vanya," he said, sitting down in the battered leather seat. He flicked off the autopilot and cast his eye over the instrument panel. Gauges and read outs were all normal. It would be a smooth landing at Althu.

He gently brought the pointed nose of the pod up and eased her over the landing pad. The blasters slowed the descent and allowed her to rest easily on her tripod feet. Immediately he felt a jerk as the conveyor belt pulled the vessel into the parking bay, out of the weather. He grabbed his leather gloves and put them on. His leather jacket fit snugly over his muscles, but provided a layer of warmth against the icy blast of air he would encounter between leaving the pod and entering the castle walls. Kelvaras looked at the helmet on the shelf as he stood by the door, noting the small camera mounted on the visor. Having a record of the conversation might not be a bad thing. He tucked the helmet under his arm and waited for the vessel to stop moving before opening the door.

Yes, that icy blast. It still managed to find the skin between his jacket and trousers. It always did.

He marched to the door, his identity card at the ready. As the vessel came to a jerking halt, he opened the door and walked down the ramp.

The Crown City of Althu wasn't a city; more a large castle, built entirely of ice rock. Kelvaras walked down the corridors to the main entrance, noting the poor repairs done to the walls and floors. The city had been invaded by Ch'ar and his army five years previously. Apparently the D'Authian Guard had walked out, letting him have the City. He shook his head – how had they not seen it coming?

His footsteps echoed loudly down the small, winding corridor. It once would've been beautiful with the large crystal chandelier high in the ceiling, but only a few of the lights were going; the other bulbs were blown and had not been replaced. Ch'ar had really let the place deteriorate.

Kelvaras looked at the large ornate doors which led to the Throne room. He paused, gathering his thoughts, preparing to meet with Ch'ar. He closed his eyes and imagined how the meeting would go.

It's been a while.

He'd avoided working for Ch'ar for some time. His last assignment had been profitable, but Kelvaras didn't like the man, didn't like his methods.

He took a deep breath, positioned his helmet under his arm, checking that the red light blinked twice before going out. Satisfied, he pushed the door open.

He marched up the carpeted aisle to the dais, where the grizzled, grey-haired man draped himself across the throne, attired in a large, black fur coat, the feeble light glistening off some of the individual fibres.

"Ch'ar," he said, pulling his hand from the leather glove and holding it towards the man. Ch'ar straightened himself up on the throne, then stood and came down the steps. He clasped Kelvaras' extended hand and shook it vigorously.

"A pleasure, Kelvaras." A genuine smile pulled on Ch'ar's features.

"Don't smile at me, it isn't natural on you," Kelvaras said.

Ch'ar threw back his head and roared with laughter, startling him.

"A man after my own heart. You smile rarely?"

"I find little in life to smile about, except the transaction."

"And direct, too." Ch'ar extended his arm and pointed to a table set up within an alcove. A large fire blazed next to it.

Kelvaras placed his helmet and gloves on the table then held his hands before the fire; once warmed, he turned to face the table. Ch'ar pulled out a chair and sat down, wrapping the cloak around him tightly as he did so.

"Shall we discuss business, then?"

Kelvaras nodded.

"There's ten in this case. There will be another twenty when you have finished the task. And if you bring me the entire army, you'll also earn another ten reward."

"Ten? I hope you are talking about millions. That's the original contract."

"Indeed it is. The ten million is in there, here is the card." He held up a small triangle, not much bigger than his thumb nail.

Ch'ar pushed it into the slot on the case. A red light outlined the card and flickered before he heard the clips inside the case disengage. The top popped, and Ch'ar pulled it open to show Kelvaras the notes stacked neatly inside.

"Why you insist on such an old fashioned payment method, I do not know. I could have this put on a card for you now, if you want the credit."

"No, this suits my needs," Kelvaras said, his tone smooth and engaging. He snapped the lid of the case shut, and elevated out the triangular card. He didn't want anyone accessing his account, less chance of payments being reversed then.

"Who am I looking for?" Kelvaras asked.

"The D'Authian guards. I understand that the commander is Vyvica Karala. She was appointed after the unfortunate death of Deverau."

"Vyvica Karala?"

"Have you heard the name?"

"I might have. What do you want them for?"

"My researchers found records and determined that the dead Queen had only one issue, a girl. The princess, though, appears to have dropped off the face of the earth. I believe she is still alive, because there are no death records. My suspicion is that the D'Authian guards fled with the princess when I invaded. They're protecting her. I need her."

"What do you need her for? Surely you can rule this planet on your own"?"

"When I invaded this deity-forsaken planet there was a hue and cry, but they were only a small voice in the Federation compared to my large input. This is another vote in my favour. With this small planet, I can finally have the majority vote at the Intergalactic Senate. They will listen to me and what I have to say. As the ruler of four planets and two planetary systems, I'll have a very big influence.

"This planet is rich with resources I can mine and sell to the other planets, and make money from them. Far more than I can on the black market.

"If I marry the princess, then there will be less opposition to my having invaded the planet. Besides, Madame Waye, the Head of the Intergalactic Senate, is insisting that I produce the princess in order to verify my claim to the throne." He gritted his teeth, clenched his fist a couple of times before turning to address Kelvaras once more. "

"Oh." Kelvaras looked down at his hands. The bearded man before him had visions of grandeur. "What makes you think the princess will marry you?"

"If she doesn't, I'll dispose of her. No apparent heir's, then I am able to legally take over the principality."

Kelvaras knew the man to be ruthless, but the death of an innocent didn't sit well with his conscience. He hoped the girl had already died. "And where do you think are they based?"

"They could be in any of the underground cities, we have canvassed the above ground cities."

"Don't bother." Kelvaras held up the screen of his vid-com and showed Ch'ar the message.

"Kelvaras Mason, this is Tyron Kwin, We have need of your services, would you please contact me immediately via return vid-com to discuss the situation and terms of agreement."

"Well, isn't that a coincidence. You do have luck on your side, Mr Mason. I will have the remaining twenty million sitting on this table for you when you return."

"Thank you."

"Out of curiosity, where are they based?"

"If I told you that, you wouldn't need me, now would you"?"

"A man after my own heart." Ch'ar chuckled.

"No, one who trusts no one."

"Fair enough. Best you get going then."

Kelvaras picked up his helmet and tucked it under his arm. Pulling the gloves on he stood up, bowed slightly at Ch'ar, then reached out for the suitcase. Ch'ar slapped a hand on top of it, preventing Kelvaras from removing it from the table.

"I want them back here, you won't get the rest unless you do." The coldness in his tone made Kelvaras shudder involuntarily.

"I don't intend to backstab you. I go with the highest bidder. Just hope that you've bid higher than they have."

Ch'ar actually smiled again. "You have more in common with me that you know, young man."

Kelvaras just nodded and tugged the case out from under Ch'ar's hand. The money would come in handy; he would send it through to his mother as soon as he could access the bank transfer system.

He turned his back on the man and walked out of the throne room, the prickling between his shoulder blades anticipating a blow that didn't eventuate.

This job could be an extreme balancing act.

CHAPTER THREE

Kelvaras had arrived late the previous night at the Port of Apos, the above ground terminal. Despite opting to stay at the Port overnight, he had done preliminary investigations and found that no one knew where the D'Authian Guards were based, nor did he know how they would meet him.

He knew that the Underground City of Apos was poor. It had been one of the jewels in the crown of the ice planet, but it had fallen on hard times since the takeover of the Crown City, as evidenced by the graffiti lining the walls and litter on the side of the entrance way instead of being picked up and disposed of properly. Some people shuffled around, hunched up in blankets against the cold, others had their feet barely covered by at least two pairs of socks, holes in one showing through different coloured pair underneath. A child ducked and weaved between legs, running on blackened stubs as he evaded hands grasping at him trying to stop him. Yelling further down the alley revealed that the young urchin had stolen some food from a bakery. Kelvaras shook his head as he headed towards the Portside Café.

Taking an outdoor seat, he studied the view through the cold deflecting glass protecting the gateway, hazed as another blizzard closed in outside.

His drink arrived at the table and he took a sip of the hot, thick, syrupy coffee, and went back to reading the latest news download.

A strong slap hit his back, spilling the hot liquid across the table.

"If it ain't Mason," said a gravelly, harsh voice. Kelvaras closed his eyes, knowing immediately who it was. He didn't turn around to confront them, there wasn't any point.

"Hello, Keme, and I presume you have your pet, Haim, with you."

A forceful kick knocked the stool out from underneath him at the same time as he stood, flicking the dribbling coffee off his fingers. The brothers were trying to make him fight, but that was the last thing he wanted to do here. He turned towards Keme, holding his hands up so they could see them.

"Come on boys, sit and have a drink with me."

Another blow hit him, this time in the base of his back, near his kidney's. Anger wasn't rising, it took over.

He spun around fast, toppling the neighbouring stool onto the toes of Haim, who swore loudly as he hopped around.

"Now look here boys. I'm trying, *really hard*, to keep calm, for both of our sakes. If you want to fight, let's take this somewhere quieter and out of the public eye." He nodded towards the security camera' surveying the open area.

"Don't really mind how and when we do this, but now's good," Haim said, a large fist aimed straight at Kelvaras' face. He leant backwards enough for the clenched fist to whistle past. Keme aimed a blow at his chest, but he jumped backwards, the fist just touching him, the impact lost by the extra distance it had to travel.

"I guess talking about this is out of the question?"

"Too late to talk," Haim said, his voice matching his brother's in gruffness.

Kelvaras sized them up.

Both were as tall as him, but both were heavier, although most of it was fat rather than muscle. He knew that he would not beat them in a brawl, which they seemed determined to start. He moved away from the table, watching for any movement from the two men standing opposite. Haim wore a patch over one eye, the result of a skirmish they'd previously had. Probably the reason for this bit of revenge.

They circled each other as patrons scrambled out of their way, picking up their plates and moving back inside the building, keen to avoid upsetting their own meal. The three men skirted around tables and chairs, kicking them out of the way.

Neither of the two men were armed, which suited Kelvaras. He preferred hand-to-hand combat; somehow the win seemed more gratifying than shooting someone point blank.

Determined to remain out of their reach long enough for the authorities to arrive and arrest them, he danced on the balls of his feet, fists raised, chin tucked.

"Can't believe you just walked into our turf."

"Didn't realise that you had marked this as your territory, I wondered why it smelt so bad here." Kelvaras could not help himself. He blinked, which was long enough for the brothers to take action. Grabbing each other's forearm, they ran at him. Unable to duck in time, their beefy forearm's caught him in the throat. His windpipe closed as it took the brunt of the blow and he fell backwards onto the frozen earth. The wind wheezed out of him, and pain racked his body. They grasped his arms and pulled them above his head followed by the sensation of being dragged. When the stars cleared from his vision, he saw he was being pulled clear of the furniture of the cafe so that the brothers could finish him off.

He used all the strength he had to pull their arms together. Their heads banged with a dull thud, but it didn't knock them senseless like he'd hoped. It did give him a moment to pull his arms free and manoeuvre onto his feet. The brothers rubbed their sore spots as they glared at him.

Not one to wait to see what would happen next, he punched out at the closest one, a blow to the stomach, just below the solar plexus. It had the desired effect and Haim went down, clutching his stomach and groaning. Keme wasn't quite so easy to fell and he had recovered enough to deflect the punch that Kelvaras threw at his nose. He wanted to try a flying kick at the man, but he couldn't risk getting winded again, because he knew that Keme wanted that. They knew him too well; if he couldn't breathe, he couldn't take them both on.

What Keme didn't expect was the feint punch to the face and the knee to the groin. Keme's eyes crossed and he toppled over backwards, thrashing, holding his groin. Neither of the brothers moved, so Kelvaras dusted his hands off and turned, in time to see Tyron clapping his hands, slowly, a sneer on his face.

"We needed someone who could be discrete. I guess you aren't the man for us." He turned and left. Kelvaras cursed under his breath as he rushed after Tyron.

"That was unexpected, and I tried everything I could to diffuse the situation."

"If that is how you 'diffuse a situation' then you definitely aren't the man we're after."

"When the authorities arrive, ask them, they have it all on screen. I was attacked first."

"Yes, and you ended it. I have been watching you, since you arrived yesterday."

Kelvaras opened his mouth to say something, but closed it again. He hadn't expected his arrival to arouse interest.

"Well, since you don't need my help, I may as well leave."

"Sounds good to me." Tyron turned and marched back to the elevator bank. Kelvaras stared at his back. He wasn't used to being walked away from. When people wanted his services, they generally begged him to work for them. Rejection wasn't what he'd anticipated. He needed the job to infiltrate the D'Authian guard, so he loped after Tyron.

"What if I drop my fee?" he whispered, walking slightly behind the tall, dark-skinned man.

"I don't think you're in a place to negotiate now." Tyron nodded towards the vehicle pods with flashing lights coming up from the Underground City. Kelvaras felt a rush of adrenaline. He didn't want to hang around and be quizzed by the authorities. In most states and planets he was a wanted man. Here, while they knew who he was and helped him occasionally, sometimes they would place a bounty on his head. He wouldn't put it past Ch'ar to do that, now that he knew Kelvaras would be liaising with the D'Authian Guard. It would save a final payment. "Just let me get in the elevator with you," he said, using Tyron as a barrier between him and the authorities.

Tyron did not respond, but when the elevator doors opened, he gestured for Kelvaras to enter. The doors closed and Tyron used his identity card to select the level he wanted.

"Thank you," Kelvaras said, relief flooded his system.

"Don't think that this is an acceptance of your terms and conditions. As I said, you're no longer in a position to negotiate."

"Oh, I think there's some room."

Tyron raised an eyebrow at the man, a smirk pulling at the corner of his mouth.

"What's so funny?" Kelvaras asked. The hissing sound he'd heard and assumed to be the elevator engine, got louder. Tyron pulled a mask up to his face.

"Crap." Kelvaras swore as his vision faded, his sense of reality distorted and dizziness caused him to reach out for something to hold himself up on. He slumped on the floor of the elevator, consciousness slipping away from him as his brain desperately tried to keep him awake.

CHAPTER FOUR

Vyvica stood over the sleeping form. Taller than she expected, taller than herself and she towered over most men.

"This is the famous Kelvaras Mason?"

"Yes, a shame really, about that fight up there. We'll have to keep him down here for a while, until the heat blows over. No doubt they'll have already identified him."

"I wonder why he accepted the job?" she asked.

Tyron laughed. "I couldn't believe how easy it was to get him here. When the authorities arrived, he was desperate to get in the elevator with me."

Alarm bells rang in Vyvica's head. He was keen to go with Tyron? She studied the older man. She had known him for as long as she could remember. He'd always been part of her life in the Crown City. If she didn't know him so well, then she wouldn't trust him with her life.

"He seemed keen to stay out of trouble with the authorities," Tyron offered in explanation, as if reading her mind.

"Mmmm," she replied. It didn't still the bells, but it made sense. She hadn't been happy with Tyron's suggestion, but Kelvaras was supposed to be the best.

"I just don't like it. I don't like inviting a stranger into our midst."

"I know, but we really don't have much choice."

The body on the cot stirred and a hand rose to his head. Eyelids flickered and Vyvica saw a glimpse of golden-brown pupils behind thick black lashes. He still wasn't quite awake, that could take a while, but she knew that the gas would make him extremely thirsty.

"Might pay to get him a drink," she said to Tyron. He cocked an eyebrow at her, but she glared at him in turn.

"It's not wise for you to be here while the negotiations take place. Or even when he wakes up. There is a bounty on your head. He could be here to collect that bounty for all we know."

"That's funny, you were just telling me that he was the best there is, now you tell me he could be here to cash in on my bounty? Which is it? Besides, he's a bounty hunter, he'll sell his soul to the highest bidder," she reminded Tyron.

"You have done your homework, Vyvica."

"Too right. We can't be too careful these days." She flicked her hand at him. "Water?"

Tyron smiled as he left the room.

It gave her an opportunity to study the unconscious man. His hair was close cropped, not shaved, little more than stubble though. A scar marred his cheek, but it didn't render him ugly. She wondered how he got it, and her fingers twitched, wanting to stroke the jagged line. With his eyes shut, and his face at ease, Vyvica thought him handsome. She smirked as she continued to study him.

He worked out, or at least he was fit, because he had a strong, muscular physique. Better than some vigilante's she had seen.

The door opened and she blushed as she pushed herself away from the cot. Tyron returned with a tall glass filled with filtered water.

Kelvaras appeared to be having some kind of dream in his half awake state, his eyelids flickering and his mouth twitching.

"Mason!" Tyron yelled at the man in the cot. Kelvaras' golden eyes opened and he stared at the two figures standing over him. He scrambled backwards, nearly toppling the cot.

"Kelvaras," Tyron said again, quieter this time.

"I didn't do it, whatever it was." Kelvaras stammered. Vyvica stifled an urge to giggle at his response. Just how many crimes was he guilty of?

"It's all right, Kelvaras. It's Tyron."

"Tyron?" They watched as his eyes adjusted to the light and he looked from one to the other. Once he recognised Tyron, his eyes flicked to Vyvica, his gaze going down her body and back up. An arched eyebrow and a slight nod made heat rise up her chest and warm her complexion.

"Here, have some water." Vyvica thrust the glass towards Kelvaras, slopping the contents. Anything to distract his stare.

He looked at the glass, then his gaze returned to her and Tyron's face "How can I trust you? You've already gassed me."

"Only because we couldn't risk having you spill the beans about our lair," Tyron said. Vyvica had to contain the laughter welling inside of her. She knew the situation was serious, but the voice that Tyron used wasn't one she was familiar with. Tyron glared at her. She ducked her head, and tried to straighten her face.

"Just drink up, it will ease the fuzziness." Vyvica indicated the glass that he now held in his hand. "For goodness sake, you would already be dead if we were going to poison you." She used the rising irritation to temper her joviality from earlier.

"True," he said, he lowered his lashes as he contemplated the glass. "And who are you?" He stared at her.

"Commander Vyvica," she replied as Tyron opened his mouth. That was all she wanted him to know, for now. "Oh for goodness sake!" Vyvica grabbed the glass from his hand and took a mouthful herself. She thrust the glass back at him, spilling the water onto his shirt.

"Thanks," he said, snarling and brushing the water off.

"Oh, it bites."

"Knock it off, the both of you!" Tyron bellowed. He looked from Vyvica to Kelvaras. Kelvaras had the sense to duck his head, but Vyvica held his stare. She didn't appreciate being spoken to in that tone. She was the commander of this outfit. Tyron held her gaze, she knew he was willing her to be quiet. She barely nodded and Tyron relaxed.

"We need your services. We have a leak and need it fixed," Tyron stated.

"A plumber would better fill your needs."

Vyvica glared at him.

"Not that sort of leak." Tyron stated a little louder to get the man's attention. "We're losing people and information. We need someone with your skills to find the source and report back to us."

Kelvaras took a mouthful of water. Vyvica hoped he contemplated their offer and wasn't trying to find something funny to say. His humour grated on her already.

"Find the source, weasel out the rat," Vyvica said, as Kelvaras opened his mouth to speak.

"Yes," Tyron said, taking over.

"Shouldn't be too hard to do."

"Good, we will pay you the requisite ten million up front, and ten million when you find us the person or persons responsible."

"Twenty mill when I find the mole."

"No deal. I told you earlier, no negotiation. You lost that opportunity when you wanted to walk away. We need help, but not that desperately." Tyron stood with his hands on his hips, his face a study in seriousness. His eyebrows were drawn down over his eyes. Vyvica recognised the 'don't mess with me' stance he'd perfected from years of dealing with her.

Vyvica watched Kelvaras carefully. He filtered the information and his face lost its humour, and the twinkle in his eye extinguished. He appeared to be seriously considering their offer, even though they all knew it was too low.

"Fifteen," he countered.

"Ten. Take it or leave it." Tyron shrugged. Kelvaras looked between Vyvica and Tyron. His face so closed Vyvica couldn't tell what he was thinking.

"Agreed. Provided I'm given protection whilst working in Apos. There are some unsavoury characters around here ready to collect my bounty."

"You! Ha, you know who I am? I think the bounty on me would be bigger than yours any day." Vyvica leaned back against the bench, crossing her arms and looking down her nose at him.

"Yes, but my bounty is dead or alive. Last time I looked, yours was alive."

"So, you do know who I am." Vyvica said, nodding.

"Vyvica Karala, the commander of the D'Authian Guards."

Vyvica turned on her heel and marched out of the room, determined to protect her dignity while she still had it. This man was able to rile her without saying much.

She didn't like the way he looked at her either. She had reprimanded men for such looks. She would have to make herself scarce around him. But she couldn't forget the heated look in his eyes as he gazed over her body. Need swelled up within her, and she pulled at the collar of her shirt to release the pressure.

Kelvaras sat on the edge of the cot after Vyvica left. Her long black hair, her dark eyes, pale sepia-coloured skin and beautiful bone structure haunted his memory. A stunning and exotic woman, even if she wore men's styled clothing.

She certainly wasn't what he'd expected with a name like Vyvica Karala. He expected someone who sat on their arse and told everyone what to do, not the athletically muscular beauty that had stood before him. And her face transformed when she smirked. A sparkle lit up the corner of her eyes when she found humour, and she had, several times throughout the conversation, but he'd managed to unnerve her.

Staring her up and down had made her blush and fidget, something that made this woman more attractive than any he had seen before. Most would take his appraisal as approval and start flirting, but Vyvica was a different type of woman, a strong woman, someone he didn't normally engage with. He liked his women small, petite and easy. Strong, tall women tended to try and take charge. He preferred to be the leader, the dominant one in the relationship.

But then he'd never backed down from a challenge before.

Vyvica looked confident and strong. He wondered what chinks he could put in her armour.

He rubbed his head and drank another mouthful of water, trying to rid himself of the arid dryness in his mouth

He hoped he hadn't snored.

CHAPTER FIVE

Vyvica and Tyron sat in the Operations Room. With the death of Agnes, they'd pulled the heads of the networks out for their own protection. They were now all housed within the warehouse complex in the lower reaches of the Underground City. With no leadership information flowing back to them, they were in limbo.

Vyvica hated being in that position, but she needed to protect her people. Someone was sabotaging her networks, and she couldn't afford to be found out for who she really was. The investigator of Agnes' line reported that it didn't appear she had given any useful information to whoever had massacred them, but there was no way to know for certain.

Even when they searched her living quarters at the Underground City of Nathe, they found nothing that would link her back to Vyvica or the D'Authian Guards. Agnes was careful. But it didn't stop Vyvica from feeling that she had put her friend's life at risk.

"Don't hold yourself responsible for Agnes' death, she knew the risks when she accepted the position, and it was a joint decision." Tyron read through the report, and guessed what thoughts tortured her mind.

"It doesn't stop me from feeling like I failed her."

"Vyvica, you didn't fail her. Her line was discovered and she was found out. We have to determine who is behind this information leak, and hopefully Kelvaras is able to do that. In the meantime, we have to get our network back up and running. We can't afford to have the line down. We don't know anything current about the situation at the Crown City. The sooner we have intel up and running, the sooner we can plan our return."

"We've been planning to get back to the Crown City for five years now. Surely we've enough information to formulate a plan. What are we waiting for?" Something prickled inside of Vyvica. Scepticism? Doubt crept in and lodged within her chest.

Tyron looked up from the papers he read. "Don't you trust me?"

Vyvica laughed. "You have to ask?"

"No, I guess not. What's really bothering you?"

"I..." Vyvica closed her mouth, trying to formulate the words before her mind ran off with her. How did she explain that the death of Agnes had shaken her fragile world, and those she'd been starting to trust were all looking like suspects. She chose another topic instead.

"Kelvaras makes me nervous. There is something about the way he agreed to take on the mission with so little payment."

"He wants protection. He couldn't go back up to the Port, it would've been too dangerous for him."

She sat back in her chair. Tyron threw the papers down on the table in front of him, unsettling her further. He looked like he was about to say something when the door slid open and Kelvaras sauntered into the room.

Without invitation he sat down in a chair and swung his feet up onto the table. Vyvica glared at him, then looked to Tyron, dropping her jaw.

"Do you have something to report?" Tyron asked him, sitting straighter in his seat as he spoke.

"Not really."

"Then would you mind explaining your interruption?" Vyvica threw at him. He turned towards her. The smirk on his face irritated her as much as the gleam in his eye.

"Oh, am I interrupting? Sorry, please continue." He clasped his hands behind his head and leaned back in the chair, his eyes appraising her body again, something behind his eyes stirred, and she recognised pure lust in them.

Vyvica raised her eyebrows at Tyron. He shook his head, but she wasn't going to take any notice of him.

Before he could say anything, Vyvica leapt across the table and straddled his lap, tipping the chair and Kelvaras backward, leaning over him, her full weight resting on her forearms across his throat. The chair hit the back wall and stayed there. Kelvaras gasped loudly as he tried to get his breath. Vyvica let the airway open just enough for him to get a little air in, but with her weight resting on his chest; he struggled to fully inflate his lungs.

"Get off!" He huffed.

"Pardon? I couldn't quite hear you?" His knees were pounding into her back, but otherwise she held him defenceless.

"Get off him Vyvica, you've proven your point." Tyron came around the table.

"Have I?"

"Vyvica!"

She turned and glared at Tyron. She didn't appreciate being spoken down to, especially by Tyron. And in front of visitors, no less.

"Get off, please," puffed Kelvaras.

"That's better," she said. Lifting her body up onto her long legs, the chair slid down the wall with Kelvaras' arms cartwheeling to keep upright. She jumped away from him before he could throw a punch at her. She landed back beside her own chair and sat down, glaring at both of the men in the room.

Kelvaras stood up, righted the chair and stood behind it. His liquid, golden-brown gaze full of amazement and anger, all directed at her. She could accept the anger and to a degree the amazement. Better than the longing and lust she'd seen in them earlier.

"I'm the commander of this group. You will address me as Ma'am, or Commander," she hissed at him. "Now, Mr Mason, do you have anything to report, or were you just leaving?"

Tyron watched her, his eyes narrowing. She directed her comments at him too, reminding him of his place.

"Sorry *'ma'am*," Kelvaras snarled.

"Ahem." Tyron stepped in, holding his arms up between them, trying to calm down the atmosphere of the room.

"Can I have a word with Tyron about the network?" Kelvaras's eyes turned cold as his eyebrows drew down over his eyes.

"That information is classified." Vyvica narrowed her gaze at Kelvaras.

"It might be, but if you want me to find your leak, you'll have to give me information so that I can work through all of the lines."

Vyvica ground her teeth together, her nostrils flaring once more. She didn't want to tell him anything. *Her* people were at risk. He was an outsider, what guarantees did they have that he would not give any of this information out once he had finished his job?

"We have safeguards in place, Commander." Tyron reminded her

"We do?" She narrowed her gaze on Tyron, but he refused to say anymore in Kelvaras' presence.

"Yes." Tyron asserted his own power in the room. Kelvaras smirked once more at the interaction between the two of them. Her feet twitched, her fingers aching to clutch his neck and clutch it tightly until he dropped to his knees, his face blue, his eyes bulging.

"This might be a part of the network's problem — miscommunication between the two head officers."

"If you aren't going to be any help then I will pack your ten million and you can go." Vyvica growled.

"Touchy."

Vyvica pushed the chair back and stood up. This time Kelvaras stood, ready for her.

"Commander," Tyron said, putting himself between the two of them. "Perhaps you should go and see what is going on in the control room."

Vyvica's anger boiled over. Tyron quickly grabbed her right wrist and pulled her out of the room. As the door slid shut she saw Kelvaras smile and wave at her.

She tried to wrestle her wrist out of Tyron's grasp, but he had a steel grip.

"Vyvica. You aren't helping things."

"Me? What about Mr wind-my-clock in there?"

"He only does it because you react. Let me handle this. I'll make sure it's recorded so that you can watch it later."

Vyvica glared at him. She opened her mouth to say something but Tyron held his hand up.

"Please, Vyvica, you aren't helping matters. Besides, we have the technology to wipe his mind once his job is finished."

Vyvica snatched her wrist out of Tyron's grasp and unconsciously rubbed it. She could see sense in what he said, and yes, they did have the technology. New as it was.

"Fine. But I don't trust him."

"Duly noted." Tyron watched her walk down the corridor to the Control Room. She heard the door open and slide shut behind Tyron as he re-entered the Operations Room.

CHAPTER SIX

A few days later, Kelvaras sidled up beside Vyvica as she headed towards the transporter.

"Where are you heading?"

She stopped walking and turned to look at him, placing her hands on her hips. "It's none of your business."

"But it *is* my business. I have to find a leak. You're going out. How do I know you aren't the leak?"

Her body tensed and Kelvaras took a small step backwards.

"You honestly think I would endanger my own networks?"

"I don't know, but I need to find out." He smirked at her as he let his shoulders drop, and slightly bent his knees. Vyvica couldn't help but smile inwardly. He was preparing for her to pounce.

Instead she turned and continued walking, hearing his shoes slapping against the concrete a few steps behind her. She pressed some buttons at the transporter and waited for the doors to open. He waited beside her.

"You can't come with me," she said flicking her hair over her shoulder.

"Why not?" he asked.

"Because then I would have to kill you."

"I don't doubt you for a minute, but I still have to go with you." His voice whispered close to her ear, and she couldn't help the shudder that passed through her and into her deepest core. Closing her eyes, Vyvica gathered her senses before replying: "On whose command?"

The door opened. Stepping inside, she pressed a button, hoping for the doors to close before Kelvaras could slip through, but he was too quick. Turning, she glared at him.

"Tyron asked me." His smug smile grated on her.

"I'll not be going anywhere while you're standing in here." The warmth growing inside of her now turned to red hot anger.

"Then we won't be going." He crossed his arms and waited.

Vyvica didn't know what to do. She had no authority over him, but by disregarding her rank as commander, he managed to rile her. Sighing, Vyvica tried to huff out as much air as possible.

The man was impossible.

"If you go with me, you have to make yourself scarce. You can't be seen to be with me, or my contact will get nervous and run. She has news that I need. Do you understand me?"

A smile of triumph lit his face. "Agreed."

Vyvica glowered at him for a moment, trying to get him to understand the implications, but he casually leaned against the wall. Using her body, she shielded the pin plate and entered the Market code without him seeing it. As soon as the last number was entered, the transporter moved sideways.

Kelvaras, unused to the inner workings of the Underground Cities, slid sideways along the wall as the cabin moved.

Vyvica didn't conceal her grin. "Sorry, forgot to say you need to hold on." She flicked her wrist in apology.

He staggered back to his feet and glared at her, his disproval evident. He brushed himself off as the transporter slowed down, then shot upwards. The motion caused him to spill forward, sprawling against Vyvica on the opposite wall. The heat of his body against hers fired desire through her, settling in her abdomen. His gaze caught hers and both inhaled at the same time. They froze, staring into each other's eyes. His irises, the most brilliant golden-brown outer with a deliciously hot chocolate centre, held her attention.

Another shift in direction jolted her to awareness and she pushed him off a little too harshly.

"Get a grip, Mason."

"I'm trying, this contraption is just a little..."

"It's just like driving a pod. You have driven pods, haven't you?"

He scowled at her. "Of course I have."

"Then counterbalance," she said, raising her eyebrows.

They stood in an awkward silence as they waited for the transporter's next move. She observed Kelvaras soften his knees and go with the sideways motion as the machine came to a halt.

The door slid open into a bustling underground market.

She watched Kelvaras look around, his eyes darting from one stand to another and his nostrils flaring, mouth-watering smells enveloping them.

Vyvica headed through the throng of people, the rabble of conversations pitched around them as customers negotiated with the vendors. Wares hung from hooks above their heads; exotic materials, animal carcasses, fresh produce, while on the benches sat fat loaves of freshly baked bread, jewellery, clothing, spices and perfumes.

Glancing behind her, she noted Kelvaras a few steps behind, his head swivelling from one stall to the next, his eyes wide. He looked at her and smiled as he hurried to catch up.

Vyvica continued pushing her way through the large warehouse sized market. Along the back wall, vendors came to the market from out of the City. One, in particular, would have some information for Vyvica, data she'd been waiting on for some time. It could answer some crucial questions and might even lead to uncovering what had happened to Agnes' network. She breathed out, trying to calm her nerves.

"You wait here, and try not to cause a commotion," she hissed as she kept her eyes on the multi-coloured stall.

An old lady flitted about like a little bird, her eyes searching every face that passed her stall. Vyvica observed her serving a customer. The old lady's head popped up from the negotiations and spotted Vyvica. She nodded, and continued her conversation. Vyvica waited to the side patiently. She glanced around, looking for Kelvaras, who worked his way along the stalls, inspecting wares and shaking his head as he moved on. Vyvica turned and when the customer left the old lady's stall, she approached. She clasped her hands together and bowed over them to the older woman. The old woman gathered her shawl about her and beckoned.

"Greetings, Commander."

"Greetings to you, Madame Jamar."

Jamar ducked her head around Vyvica, scanning the area cautiously. People collected around the stalls on either side, but no one stood close by. She indicated for Vyvica to enter the alcove behind the stall. Vyvica trusted the woman and with another glance around, ducked underneath the bench and moved out the back.

"What news do you have?"

Jamar cackled. "Always to the point, my dear."

Vyvica smiled at the woman.

"The news is that Ch'ar infiltrated one of the networks. He's feeding information down the line, part truth, testing the waters, so to speak."

"Do you know which line?"

Jamar nodded, but a commotion at the opposite stall stopped her. Her head popped up, and she looked around, her face paling. Vyvica sensed her tension and knew she would flee any second.

"Tell me, please," Vyvica pleaded. She held Jamar's gaze and opened her mouth to talk when a body slammed onto the stall bench, splintering it and crashing onto the floor.

Jamar broke eye contact and looked at the man sprawled across her counter. She turned back to Vyvica, shrugged, and leapt over the man, pushing and shoving her way through the crowd. Vyvica began to chase after her, ducking around a couple of spectators, and looking ahead, but she couldn't see Jamar anywhere. She climbed up onto a deserted stall, but the old woman had vanished. There were too many people running for her to work out where the old woman could be. Jumping down she ran back to the brawl.

Kelvaras threw a punch at a man close to him. The man countered and Kelvaras swung back, angling up and chopping him under the chin. The man's mouth clamped shut, his eyes rolled back and he fell backwards.

She didn't want to, but she had to admire his fighting style, the way his limbs moved smoothly, the flick of his fingers at the end of an extension enough to inflict a bruise, or crush a windpipe. He turned, and winked at her as he moved backwards and kicked out at another man barrelling straight at him. Her breath hitched, her heart stilling in her chest as she watched him move. A piercing siren made her look around. The spell of watching him broke, and she rushed into the fracas, grabbing Kelvaras' collar.

"What do you think you are doing?" She screamed as she hauled him backwards to a clear space.

"Watch out," he said, swinging around to kick out at a man looming behind Vyvica. She let him go and leapt aside in time for the guy to pitch forward.

"We have to get out of here." She hissed in his ear and kicked him in the rear, pushing him ahead of her.

Stallholders packed up as approaching sirens screamed. Vyvica picked up her pace, running as fast as she could through the thickening crowd, pushing

Kelvaras in the right direction. They got to the transporter just as the authorities arrived on the opposite side of the marketplace. Mayhem and panic broke out where minutes before calm, quiet negotiations were taking place.

Murmurs of discontent surrounded the arrival of the authorities, and Vyvica was surprised at how much they were detested in the underground cities. The authorities had been appointed by Ch'ar to police the various provinces, enforcing their own brutal justice. Once more she longed to recapture the Crown City.

The Transporter arrived and Vyvica, grabbing Kelvaras by one of his biceps, hauled him in. The doors closed as she dialled in the location for the warehouse. The machine took off, dumping them both on the floor.

She sat with her eyes closed, regaining her breath.

Just what the hell had he been thinking?

Twice now, he'd caused a commotion.

She raised herself onto her feet and glared down at him. He huddled in the corner, his head resting on his knees. She kicked him.

"What was that for?"

"What do you think you were doing? Do you like attracting attention to yourself?" She yelled. Her voice amplified by the confined space.

"I was trying to help."

"Help who? I lost my contact! The only information I have is what we already know, and now we don't know what's going on, thanks to your 'help'."

"There were two men trying to cheat the spice lady out of her fair share of money."

"She would've sorted it out herself. She didn't need you interfering."

His face flushed. "That wasn't what she said."

"I don't believe you. The sooner you do your job, the better." She crossed her arms and turned away from him, closing her eyes, resisting her strong instinct to beat him to a pulp, but she couldn't do that...just yet.

She imagined that when she opened her eyes he wouldn't be there. Maybe she could imagine it was all a bad dream—but that wouldn't work, she could still hear him breathing. Instead, she kept them closed until the transporter stopped.

Vyvica clambered to her feet and hurried out the door in search of Tyron, leaving Kelvaras to rise off the floor.

"He has to go!" She yelled when she found him. Tyron put his hand onto her left shoulder, trying to calm her down.

"What has he done now?"

"*He* started another brawl."

Tyron dropped his hands to his sides and sighed.

"I didn't start it," Kelvaras said as he approached them. "The other guy threw the first punch."

Tyron frowned at Kelvaras. "You seem determined to get us into trouble. Perhaps we should terminate your contract now."

"If you want." Kelvaras looked between them.

Tyron looked at Vyvica. She was conflicted. Yes, he seemed to attract trouble, and she didn't like having an outsider involved in their networks. He hadn't proved himself yet. But the feelings that he aroused in her body, the heat, the desire, the passion—she threw her hands up.

"Yes, I've had enough, your contract is terminated." She yelled over her shoulder as she headed back down the hallway, trying to push the thoughts out of her mind. She aimed for her own quarters to have some quiet time.

CHAPTER SEVEN

Tyron hadn't got rid of him, much to Vyvica's annoyance. Kelvaras had been investigating two of the local networks, looking into each person and researching each participant. So far, he hadn't come up with anything conclusive.

For two days Vyvica avoided the operations room and canteen, visiting the training room and working out instead.

Anything to evade Kelvaras.

And Tyron.

¬¬That Kelvaras remained at the facility stung. Tyron disobeyed her order.

She didn't know why, but she couldn't deny the attraction she had towards Kelvaras. It was purely physical, because heaven knew she couldn't stand his personality. The need to get out, away from the base, overwhelmed her. She needed to go and see Siara. Perhaps she could seek some comfort or solace with her. Somehow she doubted it.

Siara hadn't been shocked or surprised by Agnes death, not that she didn't expect Siara's lack of emotion. In fact, Vyvica could've sworn she'¬¬d seen a glimmer of a smile at the news, but she dismissed the feeling in the pit of her stomach.

Vyvica would've preferred taking the trip via the Intercity Transportation System to Marr. But because of the bounty on her head, and the public nature of the transportation system, she had to take the more old fashioned method of vehicle transportation.

"It's too dangerous for you to go out there on your own," Tyron said, when she told him of her plans.

"Since when have I been incapable of looking after myself?" Vyvica fired back.

Tyron nodded at her. "You have a point. Take Kelvaras with you though, you could introduce him to Siara."

"The last thing I need to do is take a six hour pod trip with that arrogant sod."

"He thinks the same about you too." Tyron smirked. Vyvica glared at him.

"Well, we might just get along since we hate each other so much. Either that or you'll find the pod crashed somewhere in the vast snow plains because we couldn't agree on which way to go."

"Sarcasm really doesn't suit you, Vyvica."

"It is all I have, I'm afraid."

Tyron put his arm around her shoulder. "You okay?"

"Yeah." She shrugged off his arm, but she knew that he cared. They had known each other for so long, and he could read her clearly. "I feel a little helpless at the moment, and I really hate the feeling. We'd planned to take back the Crown City well before now, but we've stalled. What happened? Why aren't we working on a plan?"

"The Council have yet to decide what action to take. Be patient, Vyvica, we want to make sure the attack is well thought through and planned before we go charging in. We don't want any more casualties," Tyron said.

Vyvica turned her head away. "The Council don't want to take any action. I can't handle the waiting."

"You'll have to. Besides, the Council are taking precautions. They don't want to run the risk of the princess being killed."

"Pfft, Princess," Vyvica sneered. "Agnes' death should make them consider moving things forward."

"Yes. That was a blow to our network. Hopefully we can find the cause of the breach and fix it before it's too late. But the Council aren't going to let things get out of their control. Remember Vyvica, they are the experienced ones, they know what they're doing."

"Mmmm." Vyvica didn't like the way Tyron protected the Council and their decisions. A small niggle at the back of her mind made her doubt him once more...

And Kelvaras – whether the Council approved him or not, Tyron had arranged for him to come. She didn't like that.

Or the way Kelvaras made her body feel.

"Look, take Kelvaras. You could leave him there for a few days."

Vyvica looked up into Tyron's brown eyes, noting the belief in her there. "That sounds like a good idea." She nodded and relaxed, smiling for the first time in two days.

"You never know, he might be able to pick something up while you're out that way."

"Look, Tyron, I know it's your idea, and I hope you trust him, because my gut tells me something isn't quite right."

"He's the best at what he does, just like you're the best at commanding this group."

"Flattery will get you everywhere, Tyron." She leaned into him and he kissed the top of her head, like a father would.

"I know." He smiled back. "I will contact Kelvaras and let him know. Where do you want to meet him?"

"At my pod bay?"

"He won't know where that is."

"Fine, I will collect him from his quarters."

"He isn't staying here."

"What? What do you mean he isn't staying here?"

"He wanted to stay with his vehicle."

"It's too dangerous for him to go up to the Port pod bay"."

"Yes, that's why it's parked at our pod bay, he could remain undetected there."

"I don't like it. He could leave at any time, and give away our position."

"Vyvica, you're going to have to start trusting people."

"Why? No one has done anything to make me trust them yet." She looked up at him.

"Don't be like that." Tyron growled at her. "You've known me for how long?"

She shook her head. "Too long sometimes. Tell him I'll meet him at the Operations Room, but if he's to be retained by us, then he has to stay within the compound. I don't like having a loose cannon out there. And if anything goes wrong, it's on your head, Tyron." She glared at him for impact. He nodded and bowed as she walked to the door. She paused.

"Tyron?"

"Yes?"

"Sorry, I know I can trust you, but—never mind."

"Apology accepted."

CHAPTER EIGHT

Vyvica fidgeted with her wrist communicator, uncomfortable with the whole Kelvaras situation.

What made Tyron decide to bring in an outsider?

Why did the Council accept it?

She knew that they had to approve everything that the D'Authian Guards did, but something wasn't adding up, and now... she shuddered, wondering how she would cope with six hours in a confined space with that man.

At least her personal music device would make it easier to concentrate on piloting the vehicle and keep her from listening to Kelvaras ramble on.

She marched to her room and packed some clothes into a bag. Her music device sat next to the comms console. She plugged it in, and thought for a moment. Death metal would only provoke her, but she didn't want silly ballads either. She opted for some old heavy rock classics and newer ones. The playlist downloaded in seconds and she picked it up, putting the sticky pad behind her ear. Music flooded her head, better than deafening themselves with the old fashioned ear plugs. She kept her eyes straight ahead as she hurried back to the Ops Room. It was empty, but she didn't have to wait long.

"Hello." A voice penetrated through the music in her head. Kelvaras, dressed in leather trousers and a tight, woollen top, pulled taut over muscles, casually leaned against the counter.

"Trying to impress someone?" She kept her voice flat.

"You never know who I might meet." His eyes sparkled with mischief. She liked the look, but kept the coldness in her voice.

"Let's go, fly boy." She picked up her bag and walked to her pod bay.

"You have your own private bay?" he asked, as they walked to a large hangar off to one side of the base.

She tried not to sound irritated. "I have my own entry bay."

"Oh."

He kept pace with her, but she had her eyes on her pod, a silver camouflaged machine, sleek and mean, elliptical in shape, and built for speed with small fins at the back. She pressed a button on her card and a door dropped down in a smooth motion. She entered, running her hand against the hull.

"We could take my machine," he said.

"Nope. Taking mine."

Once in the cockpit she dropped her bag into the compartment directly behind her seat and sat down, preparing the pod for departure. Kelvaras opted to take the seat next to her. His presence unsettled her but she focused on the music wildly beating inside her head, flooding her subconscious with subliminal messages to relax. Her conscious mind went through the motions of warming up the solenoids, the injectors and finally the nucleation motor itself. It hummed to life, a bare throb in the background.

Out the corner of her eye, she saw Kelvaras nod, irritating her. She turned to glare at him.

"Beautiful music to my ears," he said appreciatively. Vyvica frowned, wondering what he meant.

"The engine," he replied.

That made more sense and she could tell he was genuinely impressed. She closed her eyes, took a deep breath and let it out slowly, calming her temper, telling herself to stop over-reacting to anything he said.

"We have the finest mechanics and engineers in the southern hemisphere." The crease on her forehead eased as she looked at him. He nodded as he kicked his feet up onto the control panel and his hands went behind his head. Vyvica leaned over and pushed his boots off her panel.

"This is my baby, I don't go and plant my size eight boots all over your control panel now, do I? I would appreciate the same courtesy."

"Yes, Commander." He saluted. She closed her eyes and took another deep breath.

Don't bite, don't respond.

This is going to be a long trip.

With the vessel warmed up, she pressed a button on the dash and a large warehouse-sized panel slid sideways into the wall, revealing the exit from the pod bay. Snow drifted in soft swirls as she manoeuvred her pod, the quad feet pulling up into the undercarriage as she maintained a steady hover, moving towards the entrance.

She held the pod stable just outside, waiting for the blast door to close. The black exterior of the door was coated with thick snow that melted as the boosters reached full strength. She released the throttle and, after a moment's hesitation, the pod propelled forward at a fast rate. Kelvaras held onto his seat, inertia pushing both of them into their seats. Music blared inside her head as she made her flight checks. The white landscape blurred past beneath the pod as it raced across the vast plains of nothing. Only the hardiest of plants grew on the surface of the icy planet. The southern hemisphere was the more hostile territory, too cold and vast to be fully charted.

Vyvica flew close to the ground. She knew her vessel, it had several sensors that enabled it to move up and over any obstacles, but Kelvaras didn't know that, and she could see his knuckles whiten in a death grip with the chair, his face pale.

"Don't like speed?" she asked, raising an eyebrow at him.

"Yes, but at heights." He closed his eyes and she looked out the windscreen to see a small cliff in front of them. The vessel countered for the distance and the height and raised itself up and over the bank.

He opened one eye and looked out. Vyvica settled herself into her seat, as her chest filled with lightness. She lifted her chin a little higher as she watched the vista out the windscreen.

"Do you mind if I fly her for a bit?" Kelvaras asked.

"Yes, I do." Her face froze as she concentrated on the wall of white ahead—a solid wall of snow, blown off the ground and into the air. Snow storms played havoc with the guidance systems, not to mention the instant freeze affect it had on the engine.

"Damn."

She heard Kelvaras curse beside her. "We need to take shelter."

"There is nowhere to shelter out here," Vyvica snapped as she disengaged the autopilot, pulling the dual control stick towards her, making the pod climb. The vessel should come up high enough to avoid the snow storm.

"No, go down. Land it, now!" He shouted at her.

"What?" Her emotional control slipped and her face flushed. "My ship."

"You'll crash and kill us both if you continue this steep climb. You aren't going to outrun that wall of snow. Down. We have to land and weather it out."

She gritted her teeth. "To hell with that, Mason. I know what I'm doing."

"No you don't." He barked at her.

"What are you doing?"

"Preserving my life." He snapped, grabbing the control stick, and trying to push towards the control panel, Vyvica pulled back. The course remained steady.

"Vyvica, we don't have time. Let me take over."

"When hell freezes over," she said using every ounce of strength to pull against him. He braced himself against the seat and continued to push forward. His momentum made the nose of the pod dip dangerously fast.

If they weren't careful her beautiful machine would nosedive into the ground at speed and disintegrate, and them along with it.

Growling in anger she brought one of her legs up, and with force levered him away from the stick. She wanted to follow up with a punch, but the wall was right in front of them, she needed to act fast to save her ship. Kelvaras stepped back, shaking his head as she stood up, she realised that the only way to prevent the ship from being torn to pieces was to ease the stick forward and the vessel landed hastily on the uneven surface. Blasters stabilised the vessel until the quad feet came down.

It ground to a halt, as the wall of snow hit. Within seconds Vyvica had switched off the blasters and engine before they sucked in snow and ice, killing the engine.

Silence filled the pod as the wind buffeted against the hull. Fittingly, a low, sombre song played on the device in her head. She closed her eyes and rested on her control panel. Just breathing.

She opened to her eyes to nothing.

The vessel rocked and quivered as the snow filled wind buffeted it. She sighed and tried to collect her thoughts. She sensed rather than saw motion behind her.

Vyvica spun around and leapt through the air. Kelvaras landed heavily underneath her as she crouched on his chest.

"Never, I mean NEVER ever, touch my ship or controls again." She hissed through tight lips.

Kelvaras's face flushed red, and the next moment she stared at the ceiling with him sitting on her torso. Her breath caught at the weight of him leaning on her chest.

"Don't launch yourself at me like that unless you want to suffer the consequences."

"Consequences? I'll give you consequences!" Her eyes blazed dangerously, his image surrounded by a red haze. His eyes softened, warming as he gazed down on her. No matter how much she struggled, he kept her pinned down, his knees locking her arms to her sides. His face lowered to hers and he sniffed at her hair.

"I love the way you smell," he said. Her breath caught in her throat, her mouth went dry. She swallowed hard, trying to get the saliva back.

One hand brushed a strand of hair off her face, his fingers threading through her hair. His other hand trembled along her cheek, his fingertips leaving tendrils of fire curling into her belly.

Vyvica watched him inch forward until his mouth claimed hers. Her skin tingled with the warmth of his lips pressed against hers. His tongue probed her mouth and she opened for him. She relaxed, enjoying the heat and the sensations it stirred within her.

"Vyvica," he breathed.

Her brain registered his words, brought her back to reality, and she roughly pushed him away. He rolled off her, and landed on the floor, stunned.

She wiped her lips with the back of her hand; turning from him and 'humphing' in disgust. Her cheeks flamed with anger and embarrassment that she'd reacted to his kiss. He smiled as he climbed off the floor.

Vyvica's hand tingled with the desire to wipe that smile off his face. Her fingers twitched with the need to throttle him. But something hot ran through her blood as they gazed at each other, a reminder of his mouth lingered on hers, and she reached up a shaking finger to touch her bruised lips. She couldn't take her eyes away from his lips, and he couldn't seem to keep from gazing at her. A moment passed before he broke eye contact.

"Oh look, the wall has passed." He turned, breaking the spell between them. She hadn't noticed that the sound of the storm had eased. She hadn't wanted to take her eyes off him, but he pointed at the windscreen.

She glanced over the controls. Layers of snow blocked the view, but it was lighter than it had been moments before, and the pod no longer moved from the force of the wind. She edged her way over to her control panel and hit a couple of buttons.

Her stare was like shards of ice aimed at him. She could no longer trust him, or herself. He seemed to be after one thing. Something she could not- would not- give. The memory of his body, pressed against hers sent a tremor of delight through her, but she couldn't let her emotions run away.

She had to rein them in.

Moving away from his golden gaze, Vyvica concentrated on getting the vessel heated, to defrost the snow and ice, and get back in the air.

Marr just wasn't close enough.

CHAPTER NINE

He moved toward the back of the cabin and watched Vyvica. Her feline stealth had got him again. She could move with such lightning reflexes that she scared him. And thrilled him at the same time. Her body on his...She hadn't been prepared for the kiss.

Neither had he, for that matter.

But she'd responded, before she threw him off.

And that was where his confusion came from: she didn't react like most females; they usually melted into him and allowed him to do whatever he pleased.

Vyvica became the ice queen personified. He smirked as he thought of her ice cool exterior, no doubt the same temperature as the outside of the pod, which slowly cleared of ice.

His own reaction had surprised him too. He didn't normally feel so hot and jittery afterwards. She was supple and spry, and images of her naked flitted through his mind. He was normally the one in control – cool, calm, confident, but when she had kicked him off, he hadn't expected to feel a small sliver of loss wedge into his heart. The tension he had felt in her arms told him she was well muscled. She could handle herself in any situation, and he wouldn't be at all surprised if she had some hand to hand kills notched on her leather belt.

But was she vulnerable?

Did the ice queen have a heart there?

Could she allow anyone in to protect her?

Kelvaras contemplated sitting back next to her in the copilot seat, but with the deathly stares she kept sending his way, he knew he didn't want to get within a five foot radius. But he couldn't stand at the back of the cabin all day.

He could see that having her back to him cost her dearly, and as much as he wanted her to squirm, he didn't want to have a knife in his heart.

"I'm sorry," he said, moving slowly around until he stood in her peripheral vision.

"Mmmm," she said.

He had to bite his tongue.

There were so many ways he could retaliate, but he didn't want her springing to her feet again.

He continued to slowly edge around until he slid into the copilot's seat.

"I said, I was sorry."

"I heard you the first time."

"It is customary to acknowledge the apology."

"I know it is."

"And to apologise too."

Her hazel eyes pierced him with their steeliness.

"You nearly crashed my pod. What do I need to apologise for?" Her eyes communicated that she wanted to say more. But she didn't bring up the kiss. His heart raced as he thought about it.

Bite your tongue screamed through his mind.

"You could apologise for kicking me off you and trying to kill me." He closed his eyes; mentally kicking himself.

He didn't need her to hit him again.

"I wasn't trying to kill you. I could do that if I wanted to." She blinked rapidly as she spoke.

"I don't doubt you." He rubbed his chest, tender to the touch. He could imagine the bruises that would grace his torso tomorrow.

He watched as she checked the sensors. Orange lights glowed on the dash, each button blinking to green, indicating the snow and ice had melted off. He watched as she started the pre-flight checks and started up the engines.

Once more the hum of a well-serviced motor filtered through the air, filling the cabin with a new energy. He studied her movements as she hit the boosters, giving the pod enough lift to pull up the feet. She gently moved the stick increasing the pressure on the accelerator allowing the pod to slowly lift off the ground. Instead of skimming over the ground, the pod rose to mid-stream, about five hundred feet above the ground.

Clear of any obstacles.

For that he was thankful.

He decided she knew how to fly, and efficiently too.

Looking back, she probably could have flown them over the snow storm. But he had decided to butt in. He shook his head, drawing a quick glance from Vyvica. He smiled at her and refocused outside. Why did he have to interrupt her? Because he wanted to save his own skin, he didn't want to die, and he thought that she was reckless.

Which she was.

Vyvica was reckless.

But he couldn't match up her recklessness with her efficiency.

He watched her sit back in her seat and close her eyes, slender hands reaching up and massaging her temples.

"Are you alright?" he asked, suddenly struck by how pale and fragile she now looked. But when she turned to glare at him, the image of a fragile flower disappeared.

She wasn't brittle or ready to break.

She was solid ice.

"I'm fine."

She obviously didn't want conversation. But he did.

"Tell me about yourself?"

"Why?"

"Because I asked."

"Not good enough reason. Tell me about you."

"Nothing much to tell."

"Same. No history or past, no future."

"That's sad."

"It's an answer. Nothing more, nothing less. Analyse it how you will."

Definitely not a conversationalist. There was no hope for him. He sighed deeply.

"There's some video chips out the back if you want to watch something." Vyvica indicated over her shoulder, her eyes not leaving the panel.

"No, the scenery is enough for me."

"Suit yourself."

He continued to stare out the window, the occasional snowflake splattering against the screen."Who's in Marr?"

"My friend."

"Male or female."

"What does it matter to you?"

"Just curious."

"You want to know way too much for my liking."

"It's my job. Knowing who we are going to meet will help me to make some connections. When you introduce me, tell them my name is Mason and I'm heading up a new network." He saw her cringe. "It's necessary for my cover. I can't have everyone knowing I'm here to find a breach in trust, because then the leak will dry up."

She remained quiet, non-responsive. She pulled up a graceful and muscular leg, resting it on a small handle below the control panel. A slight tremble showed how much tension she held in her body."Siara. We're going to visit Siara," Vyvica replied quietly.

"Siara. All right. She is the leader of the southern branch?"

"Yes."

"Good. Progress. That's good." Her brow furrowed and her eyebrows moved closer to each other and he smiled hoping it would show his sincerity. "How long have you known Siara?"

"For quite some time."

"Can you be more vague?" He winced as the barb slipped out and once more she pursed her lips and her eyes narrowed at him. "Sorry, you just bite so well, I can't seem to help but bait you. I apologise."

"I don't appreciate your humour. I don't like you. Stop with the questions."

Once more she shut him down and again, she started to massage her temples, a frown pulling at her forehead and darkening her eyes further.

"I have some tablets if you need something."

"Mmmm."

He didn't move as her response was neither affirmative nor negative.

Best just to sit still.

And wait.

CHAPTER TEN

Relief flooded through Vyvica as she saw the approach lights for the landing of the Above Ground City of Marr, the outlaw town. Since the invasion, the town had become closely affiliated with Ch'ar. While the Internal Transportation System would have genetically identified Vyvica as soon as she landed at the portal, the external ports used manual methods of identification- she could have a false name and get away with it.

Bounty hunters were frowned upon and often killed on site. A smile crossed her face as she thought about how Kelvaras might get along. But her conscience tingled.

"Got your ID?" she asked, as she lined up the pod with the navigation lights. He nodded.

"Which one?"

"Mason Deminica."

"Yes, right here," he said, waving it in his hand. She punched some buttons and waited for a small port to open to remove her ID card, one for Idia Deminica. Kelvaras had been quiet for the remainder of the journey, but she decided not to allow him the chance to talk, instead turning up the volume of her personal music device. The music drowned out her own thoughts too, as she flicked the boosters on her pod and used them to levitate across the ground easing it in between two large merchant ships and into a parking bay.

She initiated the cool down sequence and they disembarked, greeted by the authorities.

"ID's please." The authorities were a mix of Ch'ar's army and local gangs. Vyvica hated Ch'ar's authority; it was suppressive and suffocating, her smile tight as she handed over her fake identification card, encoded with fake DNA.

"Thank you Ms Deminica. And the purpose of your visit?"

She smiled prettily at the visor-clad guard and swung her bag over her shoulder. "Visiting my sister-in-law." There was an amplified sniff as the guard inspected her card and looked back up at her. The visor hid the guard's eyes, but she could imagine he had mentally undressed her.

"Well I hope you have a nice stay." The electronic voice said. as he nodded to her.

"Sir?" He turned to Kelvaras who handed over his D'Authian provided false identification chip. The guard inserted it into his handheld scanner.

"And the purpose of your visit Mr Deminica?" Kelvaras's face lit up with a smirk. She knew what was coming before it came out of his mouth.

"Here with my wife, to see my sister," he said, putting his arm around Vyvica's shoulders. She closed her eyes and shook her head in disbelief, but plastered a smile on her face as she reached an arm around his waist. She drove her nails into his shirt, satisfied with the small grunt he gave.

"And how long do you anticipate staying?"

"Long enough," Vyvica said, stepping away from Kelvaras's arm.

"Very good. Thank you." He handed the chip back to Kelvaras, who pocketed it.

The ground was rock hard, and cold under Vyvica's ice boots. She glanced down at Kelvaras's shoes and noticed that he had indoor boots on.

"Weren't well prepared, were you 'darling'," she said loud enough for the guards to hear. She heard them chuckling as Kelvaras slipped and grabbed hold of her arm.

"I would've thought that a man of your talents would've been better prepared." She smiled brightly at him, holding his hand in hers while he regained his footing.

He didn't respond like she thought he would. As soon as he righted himself, she extracted his arm from hers and marched off towards the gates and the shelter of the city.

Once inside, she moved through the maze-like alleyways, leading them deeper into the city. While it wasn't underground like Apos, roads and alleyways were covered to provide protection from the elements for pedestrians. No vehicles were allowed within the walls of Marr, except the authorities.

It took them half an hour to reach the apartment block. Kelvaras kept up with her without any problems, and she presumed that he might be familiar with the city.

Vyvica wrinkled her nose at the overpowering stench of urine and vomit in the stairwell, and the detritus that lay on the walkway along the apartment block.

She knocked on the door of an apartment, listening to the sound of stumbling and mumbling before the door cracked open and a mass of tangled dirty blonde hair and ice blue eyes stared out at them.

"What?"

"It's me," Vyvica whispered. No lights illuminated the apartment. She hoped that her voice wouldn't carry to any nosy neighbours. A loud yawn issued from the head and the door stretched as far as the security chain would allow. A pale face studied her, narrowing its eyes, before widening.

"Vyvica?" The face lit up with excitement.

"Shh." Vyvica looked around to check that no one was watching. "Just open the door."

The door closed and they heard the chain rattle. It re-opened and it took some time for Vyvica's eyes to adjust to the darkness within the foul smelling apartment.

"You live like a pig," Vyvica stated. Siara tried to close the door behind her, but a strong push against the door stopped it, creating a din in the process. Vyvica spun around scowling at Kelvaras.

"Do you have to create a scene?" She hissed. Kelvaras shrugged his shoulders, the last motion she saw of him before the door closed, shutting out the artificial light from outside.

"What is that smell?" She heard Kelvaras say with a nasally voice. Like her, he probably held a hand over his nose.

"Who the hell is this?" Siara muttered.

"Siara, meet Mason." She moved through the pitch-black room, making her way, she hoped, towards the windows. Her feet stood on uneven surfaces, and something squelched under her boot. She shuddered, not wanting to think about what it might have been. Her shin struck an obstacle and she nearly swore, rubbing at the bone as she stumbled across the room.

"Do your lights not work?" Vyvica asked as she groped along the back wall. She felt the shutters under her hand and sighed. While the security at the door was lax, the shutters were high tech.

"Can you open the blinds please, Siara," she asked. The smell was worse over this side of the room, and she had to pinch her nose to block it out. An electronic buzzing filled the space and the shutters slowly slid down the window, flooding the dank apartment in pale light. She studied the ground around her, appalled at the state of the apartment, which was paid for with D'Authian money.

"Siara," she whined. She looked over, but Siara stared open mouthed at Kelvaras.

Vyvica put her hands on her hips, taking in the image of Siara in a dirty tank top and grey brief underwear. Kelvaras studied the woman's physique too and her stomach hardened as spots loomed before her eyes. The jealousy surprised her.

"Hi." Siara smiled at Kelvaras, leaning back onto one hip, and flipping her dishevelled hair over her shoulder.

"Oy, Siara!" Vyvica called out, waving her arms. Siara looked over.

"Hi, hon, how's it going? You didn't have to bring me a present, but thank you." Her accent sharpened with interest. Kelvaras looked around, taking in the state of the room. His stare connected with Vyvica's and he conveyed to her what she already knew.

"What a dump."

"Sorry, hon', wasn't expecting visitors. Hang on." She pressed her ID card against a panel by the door, using some credit contained on it. Within seconds, the rubbish vanished. The cover on the couch still lay crooked and stained and dishes remained in the sink beside Siara, but the room no longer contained the rubbish of lazy living. Vyvica walked over to the couch and straightened the cover before she sat down.

"Thought I would drop by and see how things were going."

Kelvaras moved to a seat beside the window, pulling items of clothing from the cover and straightening it. He threw the clothes onto the floor and sat down, obviously not impressed.

The removal of the rubbish hadn't taken away the stale stench and Vyvica couldn't handle it any longer. She stood up and opened the window. Cool, cleaner air flooded into the room.

"Hey, that's cold!" Siara whinged.

"Then get dressed. We're here on official business."

"Give me a second, hon," she said.

Vyvica watched as Siara disappeared through a door on the right of the main living room. They could both hear Siara rummaging around, trying to find clean clothes.

"And she's your friend?" Kelvaras asked quietly. Vyvica glared at him, daring him to say anything, but sighed and nodded her head.

Even with the clutter gone and the window open, the smell of rotten food, unwashed clothing and sweat clung to the air. Kelvaras couldn't miss the details, his training drilled that into him, and there was something odd about this room. Despite the mess, it gave the impression that the occupant didn't actually live there. He didn't like the vibe he got from the place, but as he leaned forward to tell Vyvica, Siara came out of her room.

She slunk across the floor in a tight bodice top, and long skirt which flowed to the ground. She had a figure and knew how to use it. He raised his eyebrows, which made Siara smile and wink at him conspiratorially.

"So, what do you want to discuss?" she asked, sitting on the end of the couch between Vyvica and himself. A move neither of them missed.

"May I suggest that we go to a cafe or something?" Kelvaras looked at Vyvica pointedly.

"We can conduct the business here," Vyvica said tightly.

He sighed inwardly. "I would very much like to get away from this smell."

"No, stay. I'll fix us a nice coffee," Siara said, springing to her feet. She suddenly seemed nervous.

"I think you're right, fresh air would do us some good," Vyvica decided. It wasn't lost on Kelvaras that the air outside the building, within the city, wasn't fresh, but filtered, and had to be better than the swampy gas that floated around the room.

"The windows are open, it won't take long for the air to clear." Siara looked from Kelvaras to Vyvica. Vyvica stood, and Kelvaras took his cue from her. Vyvica flashed him a surprised look, like she wasn't expecting such resistance from Siara.

"That's settled, two against one. Let's find a nice coffee house," Vyvica said as she walked to the door and opened it before Siara could protest. Kelvaras waited as Siara sulkily grabbed a jacket from behind the door and slammed it behind them as Vyvica marched off down the walkway.

He wanted Siara to trust him, he needed her to feel comfortable around him, but he wouldn't have to try hard. Siara flashed him a smile that lit up her face. Her tight fitting jacket snuggled over her breasts, allowing a peep of flesh from the top of her bodice and Kelvaras couldn't help but look.

"Vyvica can be quite blunt, but I'm not as hard or as cold as the ice queen there," Siara said, batting her eyelashes at him. He smiled his most flirtatious smile.

"I bet. You seem quite an outgoing person."

Siara shot him a curious look, smiling in her confusion. That look confirmed his suspicions faster than anything else; that and the strange card that had been on the bench as he walked past. He recognised the crest on it, and had been surprised that someone was this close already.

Why did Ch'ar want him if he already had someone inside?

A large mug with steaming black liquid sat in front of him. He couldn't help but listen in on the conversation Vyvica and Siara were having, catching up on old times.

Vyvica laughed, and Kelvaras stared at her. Her smile radiated across her face and she glowed. She cast a glance over at him and looked amused at his expression.

She returned to Siara, but the glance had drawn the other woman's attention.

"Are you two an item or something?" Siara said, leaning forward on her seat. Vyvica snorted. The other woman looked from him to Vyvica, before finally settling her gaze on him.

"Well?"

"Nope. Nor will we ever be. I like my women feminine," he said, winking at Vyvica.

Siara laughed, but Vyvica froze. He could tell he'd hurt her with his words. It surprised him, because she hadn't shown any interest in him, other than as a punching bag.

Vyvica and Siara started talking again, and he used the opportunity to observe both women. They were so different. While Vyvica was uptight and tense, constantly on guard, Siara was relaxed and all femininity. They were also physical opposites. Vyvica had dark hair with exotic coloured skin, Siara sat playing with her fair hair, which matched her pale, washed-out skin. Her blue eyes flashed with amusement at something Vyvica said. But while Siara seemed like a fun, loving girl, Vyvica had maturity and more natural poise.

He saw that the girls were silent and staring at him. He'd missed something.

"Pardon?"

"I just asked Vyvica where you were from, Mason."

"Oh, I... ah... I'm from all over, really." Siara shot a confused glance at Vyvica, before looking back at him.

"I'm from Planet Fluut originally, but I'm a citizen of Eladora. I move from one place to another." He shrugged, hoping the answer sounded truthful.

Siara rested her face in her hands, waiting for more. Her eyes smouldered with sexiness and wanton lust. He shuffled in his seat, before returning his gaze to the women. Vyvica sat back, looking amused by his awkwardness.

"Then...why are you here?" Siara asked. Vyvica picked up her mug and closed her eyes as she took a long sip. She wasn't going to help him out at all.

"I've recently been going through my ancestry and found a link with the D'Authian guards. When I approached them, they were able to fill in gaps for me. They took me in and trained me. I've felt like part of a family for once in my life." He recited, as instructed by Tyron.

"You have no family? Oh, that is sad." Siara pursed her lips, a pretty, flirtatious pout. He wanted to roll his eyes, but resisted the urge.

"No family. I'm an orphan, but that isn't so bad."

"I guess not." She replied, smiling at him, her eyes ranging up and down his body. He tried to sit still, but the urge to get up and move grew stronger. Her hungry stares made him uncomfortable. He could see she thought of him as being a bad boy and wanted to mother him.

He hated lying.

He had a mother, who was extremely well looked after in Fluut, along with his older sister.

"So why are you guys here?"

"Mason is going to take over Agnes' network, and he needs to know the procedures," Vyvica said. He watched Siara carefully; she didn't show any sign of being upset about the mention of their dead mutual friend.

"Doesn't Tyron normally handle that kind of thing?" Siara narrowed her eyes, her gaze flicking between Vyvica and himself.

"I was coming out to catch up with you, so he thought it was a great idea for me to bring Kelvaras and introduce you two. Besides, we've been having some issues and the Council decided the best method would be for him to have some on-the-job training."

"Oh, I like the sound of that." Siara's voice went husky. Kelvaras couldn't believe how easily a lie could roll off Vyvica's lips. He could lie like a soldier, but he didn't expect the leader of professional bodyguards to be so proficient at lying.

"Siara, we need you to take him on for a week, show him how to pass information down the line, and get the information back again. I brought him here because I trust you."

Kelvaras watched Vyvica closely. She fidgeted with the cup and didn't look at Siara as she said it. He wondered if Siara knew that Vyvica didn't really mean what she said.

His mind went back to the conversation.

"Wait, a week?" Kelvaras wished that he'd known about this change of plans, he had no change of clothes with him. And he hoped that it didn't mean staying at that hell-hole Siara called a flat.

"Well, we'll have to see what we can squeeze in during that time. Hopefully I can get him up to speed. We may need an extension of time..."

"I'm a fast learner," he said quickly, feeling a cold sweat forming on his forehead.

"Good, you'll stay with Siara and Tyron will be back to get you in seven days. Siara, you have the communicator if anything happens."

"Yes."

"Don't I get one?" Kelvaras asked.

"You don't need one at this stage. You need to know what you have to do to set up a new network. Hopefully we can get that going in a week."

"Did they wipe out the entire network? Wow, that's impressive." Siara blurted out. She looked wide eyed at the two faces staring at her. "I mean, that it's hard enough for me to keep up with my own network, without knowing everyone in it. They'd have to be rather good to have infiltrated the entire network."

Kelvaras felt a cold shiver go up his spine. Something didn't feel right about this girl.

CHAPTER ELEVEN

Siara lowered her head and looked at Kelvaras from under her lashes, smiling coyly at him over the top of her coffee cup. He looked around the trashy apartment. Two nights he had spent there, and already he wanted to get back to Apos. Spending time in Vyvica's company was preferable to this. Siara scared him, and women, generally, didn't scare him.

The night was black, but she didn't rise any time before sunset. She didn't get home until well after sunrise. How she survived he didn't know. So far, she hadn't taken him on any of her excursions, explaining that she needed to warn her informants first. He somehow doubted that.

He'd cleaned up the apartment the first day as best he could, while she lay comatose. He'd also been out and brought some clothes, food and decent coffee. When she'd awoken, she came out, looked around, smiled at him and made coffee, her long blonde hair ruffled and tousled with sleep. While she thought she was sexy, and flaunted her figure, Kelvaras found it too thin and the dark smudges which circled her eyes definitely weren't a turn on.

Not that it stopped her from trying to hit on him. He'd rebuffed her and kept a distance, to which she'd told him she liked her men hard to get. He'd replied that he liked his women to have meat on their bones. It didn't seem to upset her one bit.

She'd offered him her bed, but he chose the uncomfortable couch, preferring the lumps to the confines of her musty and stuffy bedroom, or the chance of an extra body in the bed the next morning. Her bed took up all of the room, how it got in there he didn't know. The entire flat was tiny, consisting of open plan lounge, kitchen, separate bathroom and bedroom.

"What's the plan for tonight?" he asked, standing on the lounge side of the breakfast bar. Siara leaned forward, pushing her breasts together with her upper arms as her hands clasped the coffee cup, a finger circling the rim in a seductive manner.

"We're going to see my contact tonight." She licked her lips as she studied him. He tried not to shudder, sipping his coffee to hide his revulsion. Even she stank—body odour, sour milk, musty smelling clothes. Nothing about her attracted him one bit.

"Okay," he said. He moved to sit in the large overstuffed chair, waiting for Siara to get ready which he knew would take her quite some time.

"Ready?" she asked, surprising him, because she hadn't moved. He looked up at her; she hadn't changed from the previous day, skinny trousers, long-sleeved, tight-fitting t-shirt.

"Yeah."

He grabbed his thick jacket. Some of the city remained exposed to the chill, and he'd need his new winter-weight jacket. He held the door open as she pulled her own jacket on, flicking the fur lined hood up over her head.

"Thank you, kind sir," she said with a posh accent, pinching his butt. He flinched, knowing that he could've avoided that. He choked back a horrid retort, instead smiling through the pain. Her long thick nails had squeezed rather hard. He rubbed at the spot as they walked down the metal walkway to the stairs.

"Where exactly are we going?" he asked.

"You'll see," Siara said as she linked her arm through his and sauntered down the road as if he were her possession.

Kelvaras breathed through his mouth, trying to avoid smelling Siara. She probably hadn't had a shower since he arrived, but a sickly sweet odour emanated from her. He wasn't sure what it was.

Siara chatted and chirped her way along the road, occasionally calling out to a group of people who were standing around. Crowds moved into the streets at night, they were different to the ones who walked with purpose during the day. Siara led him around the maze of roadways until they came to a large building. Lights filtered out through dirty windows.

"Hey, Yan!" Siara called out as she marched up the steps. An impressively tall and big man, obviously Yan, opened the door for them, eyeing up Kelvaras. He grinned at him with what he hoped was his most charming and peaceful smile, but the gruff man held his stare, narrowing his eyes. The thought of trying to tackle him if Yan decided he didn't like him made Kelvaras shudder as he passed by.

He swallowed hard as Siara let go of his arm and walked through the thick crowd, weaving through them effortlessly. Kelvaras didn't have as much luck.

He kept his eye on the white jacket that bobbed in front of him, but it kept getting further and further ahead. The crowd seemed to open up for Siara and close behind her as she brushed through, shutting him out.

"Excuse me, pardon me, excuse me"," he murmured as he pushed his way through the crowd. He didn't like the looks he got, but he couldn't take his eyes off Siara for a moment. She disappeared and he felt the crowd closing in around him. A few menacing growls and warnings were issued, but he ignored them, hoping that was the best course of action.

"Kelvaras, honey, are you coming?" Siara called at the top of her voice. Suddenly the press gave way and a path opened up to Siara. She stood at the door way of a darker room, her hands on her hips, glaring at those around her. For once, he was grateful to Siara.

"Thanks," he muttered as he approached her.

"You're welcome," she whispered seductively into his ear. He moved quickly before she could pinch his butt again. And waited inside the door until she took the lead again, following her closely, although there were less people in this room. She moved towards the empty dance floor.

"Wanna dance?" She yelled at him over the extremely loud pumping music. The air seemed to vibrate in time with the beat, rocking his body hard and he found the sensation unsettling.

"Later?" he asked. She shrugged and looked around the room. Four statues stood in a corner.

"Come on." She pulled him towards them. Only as he approached did he realise that they were people, gently swaying, out of time with the music. It was hot and stuffy and the funny sweet smell was thicker in this corner.

"Hey, Jarha," Siara said to one of the statuettes.

"Hey." The statue replied with the minimum of movement.

"This is Kelvaras, a friend of mine," Siara said. Jarha barely nodded her head.

"Any news?"

Kelvaras would have missed the shake of the head had he not been watching. Siara looked around the room, missing the movement.

"Anything I should know about?"

"Yeah, Stott is coming."

"Stott? *The* Stott?" Suddenly Siara seemed very animated and excited.

"Yeah."

"Crap," she muttered, as she lifted her arms and sniffed at her pits. Kelvaras raised his eyebrows, but she appeared to consider her scent acceptable. She started whispering with Jarha, and ignored Kelvaras. Obviously Stott was someone of interest to her. He would have to investigate him further.

"Siara?" He tapped her on the shoulder, a look of surprise on her face. She must have forgotten he'd accompanied her.

"Hey honey, look, there's no information, and nothing much happening here, so why don't you head on home," she suggested before he could open his mouth.

"Can I talk with Jarha?"

"You could try." Even in the gloom, he could see Siara roll her eyes with impatience. He chose to ignore her.

"Jahra?" He leaned towards the stick thin woman, her face whiter than the snow, her black hair plastered to her head. She didn't look healthy and she didn't acknowledge him.

"Jahra! Can I talk with you?" He shouted over the music. It died just as he started saying it. Jahra turned her blank stare onto him.

"Don't need to yell," she responded, her voice a monotone.

"Sorry, can you tell me how you communicate with your contact?"

"That's confidential, I can't tell you."

He sighed, he tapped Siara on the shoulder. She turned her ear to him, but kept facing the door.

"Can you talk to Jahra? She won't talk to me."

"I told you she wouldn't."

Kelvaras clenched his teeth tightly, his jaw clicking in irritation.

"Go home, Kelvaras, there's nothing here for you." She pressed the entry chip into his hand. "Don't wait up for me," she smirked at him and winked.

If they weren't in such a public place, Kelvaras would've slapped her across the face. How dare she dismiss him like that.

He crossed the dance floor and stood at the doorway, looking over at Siara. She puffed on a pipe, laughed, then stood stock still. Someone pushed him from behind. He turned to say something, but the man had already brushed passed. He was tall and muscular, almost the same size as the bouncer at the door. His head was shaved and covered in tattooed swirls.

Kelvaras watched as the man walked over to Siara. The big man picked her up, squeezing her in a bear hug, then threw her over his shoulder and exited through a door behind where they had been standing.

Kelvaras took some pictures of them on his comms unit before taking a step in their direction, but another man tapped him on the shoulder. He tucked the comms unit into his pocket as he turned to see who was behind him. A thin, muscular man indicated for him to leave. Kelvaras considered his options. Stay here, start a fight and end up in the authorities custody, or leave and do some research on this Stott character.

He had no choice.

In a way, he was pleased to be escaping the room. The confined space and the sticky, sweet smell made his stomach turn and he hurried to navigate through the main bar. The men eyed him as he headed towards the entrance, most stepped aside for him. He hoped it was Siara's influence that convinced them to leave him alone, but he didn't think she had enough sway. She thought she did, but it was probably the big guy behind him, shadowing him as he left the building, making sure he left unimpeded.

Relief flooded through him when he finally got back outside into the chilled night air without a black eye or punched kidney. Yan eyeballed him as he exited the door.

"Best thing for you, little man," the bouncer said and spat, the globule landing by Kelvaras' feet. For once, he ignored the jibe and instead let the blast of cold air refresh him. He glanced at Yan, waving as he left.

Disappointment surged through him as he walked back to the apartment. He had wanted to find something on Siara, something in his gut told him that she wasn't all she made herself out to be.

How she and Vyvica ever became friends really baffled him.

CHAPTER TWELVE

Kelvaras opened the door to the apartment and the musty smell assailed him. He stepped back onto the landing, holding a hand over his nose. Taking a deep breath, he hurried across to the opposite side of the room and threw the door open onto a tiny balcony.

He stood out there, gasping fresh cold air into his lungs, not worried about the coldness condensing around him. The door pinged back off the window frame, but didn't shut. Taking a deep breath, he hurried back inside, throwing open all of the windows in the lounge. The cold air slowly seeped in and he inhaled, appreciating air that wasn't hot and stuffy. A swirling cloud of mist formed outside the window as the warmer air met with the cold.

He looked around the lounge. Although he'd straightened it two days ago, he wouldn't have guessed it to look at it. The place needed a good spring clean. Even the plant that sat on top of the sound system looked near death.

Kelvaras picked it up, muttering under his breath as he sat it in the sink and turned on the tap. Water poured straight through the pot, but the soil started to swell.

He went back to the lounge and pulled the blanket off the couch, shaking it out on the balcony. A cloud of dust joined the mist that rolled off into the night. The couch wasn't pretty and he quickly covered it again, carefully tucking the blanket in behind the cushions. He pulled the cover off the lazy boy chair and something large fell onto the floor. He looked down at the communicator and studied it carefully before picking it up.

An imported one, not widely available on the planet. He dropped the blanket as he turned the small black box over in his hand. There was no screen visible on it. He pushed at a button on the side and a soft whirring vibrated the communicator in his hand. Turning it over he saw two small doors slide across to reveal the screen.

He moved his fingers over the display, lighting the screen as he touched it. He found several recorded messages in a secret part of the programming, obviously something set up by the person who had given it to Siara. He went through, listening to snippets of conversations.

His face went pale and the hairs on the back of his neck rose as he listened to them.

Using the small touch panel, he called the last number. A hissing noise issued from the unit as it waited for connection before he heard a voice at the other end.

"Yes, Siara," said an impatient voice.

A voice he recognised.

A chill went through him as he realised what was going on.

"Ch'ar, I shouldn't be surprised should I?"

"Who is this? This is a secure connection."

"It's Kelvaras."

There was a pause. "Ah, Kelvaras."

Kelvaras waited for further confirmation, but the communicator remained quiet.

"I have just exposed one of your agents. You didn't tell me you had more than one person on this job." His voice remained low, cold. If he had two people on the job, there could be more.

"I guessed that. And how's your progress going?" Ch'ar asked.

"I'm working on it. You'll have some information soon enough." He paused, unsure what to say next. "I shall have to pass this information on to the D'Authian Guards."

"She has outlived her usefulness. And yes, I'm counting on you giving that to them. Don't worry, dear boy, you're the only vigilante I have called in. Siara was useful at the time, but she hasn't given me anything I didn't already know."

"Why will it work in your favour?"

"If you won't tell me where they are..."

Kelvaras thought through the implications. The comms unit would have a tracking device in it.

"Do you want me to deliver them or not? If you come crashing in, I'll forewarn them. I know you don't like my style, but you could at least let me do this my way."

The other end of the communicator remained silent. Then an audible sigh. "I suppose I'll have to let you do it *your way*."

"Thank you." Kelvaras' mouth went dry and his stomach skittered with nerves. Something wasn't quite right about this. Ch'ar wasn't known for giving up quite so easily.

"Have you any news to report?"

"Only that Commander Karala is a hard lady to be with. I'll endeavour to have her to you by the end of the lunar month." Kelvaras swallowed, hoping his voice didn't betray his lie.

"Okay then."

The communicator went dead, Ch'ar signed off without a farewell.

Being familiar with this type of communicator, he quickly erased his communication before working on deprogramming the positioning beacon. He went through every inch of the internal workings, spending considerable time to make sure that there weren't any extra tracking mechanisms set into the machine.

Once he had reassembled it, he sat on the couch, looking at the contraption in his hand. He didn't know how he would tell Vyvica, she would be shocked by the information that he had here in his hands. She'd already lost one friend, now she could possibly lose another.

He shook his head, what did it matter to him?

It surprised him that it mattered a lot.

CHAPTER THIRTEEN

It hadn't been her idea to retrieve Kelvaras.

In fact, Vyvica had hoped they'd transport him, but there were no reliable links with Marr, not without giving their own position away. But that didn't explain why Tyron insisted she go and collect him. He was just as available as her. Her anger smouldered as she considered the journey back in his company.

She closed her eyes. Why? Why did he have to come back so soon? She'd survived the week incredibly well not having him around, able to relax and be carefree, not having to watch her every move.

Her thoughts moved to Siara, excitement at catching up with her friend. She hadn't heard anything from her for the entire week. A nerve twitched in her cheek and her stomach flittered as she considered what Siara and Kelvaras might've gotten up to.

Siara had definitely been all hot and heavy for him, especially when she found out that Kelvaras and her weren't an item.

Had he succumbed to her desires?

Something hot seared through her; anger perhaps?

Couldn't be anything else, could it?

Vyvica arrived at Marr in good time, passed by the authorities and made her way to the apartment. Kelvaras answered the door, his face drawn.

"You're a sight for sore eyes." He sounded genuinely pleased to see her. She raised her eyebrows, but he smiled and opened the door wider and moved to hug her. She tried to side-step him, but he grasped her. Standing stock still, she allowed him to place his arms around her, but she glared at him as he let go.

"It's been a hell of a week. Just pleased to see a friendly face," he said by way of explanation. She wasn't convinced.

"Where's Siara?"

"Asleep," he whispered as they moved into the lounge. She eyed the flat, noting it smelled better and was tidier than her last visit.

"I really need to talk to you, privately," he whispered.

Vyvica studied his face, concern etched at the corners of his mouth and his hands fidgeted with the hem of his shirt. He looked anxious. And it unsettled her to see him nervous.

"Just spit it out."

"Can we go somewhere else and talk?"

"Can you not say it here?"

His anxiety piqued her interest as he grabbed a jacket and opened the door for her. She exited and stood on the walkway waiting for him.

"What's going on?"

"She's the leak, Vyvica."

"I beg your pardon?"

"I saw it the first day we were here, but I've found more evidence."

Her eyebrows drew together. "It'd better be damned good, Mason." She marched off down the walkway, wanting to put some distance between herself and the apartment. Kelvaras ran to keep up with her.

Settled at an outdoor cafe, drinks in hand, he finally spoke.

"Siara was the one that provided information to some of Ch'ar's army. They were the ones that wiped out Agnes' network."

"Why would she do that?"

"She didn't like Agnes. You know that. But it went deeper than that, deeper than jealousy, and Agnes could see through her. Siara is in direct contact with Ch'ar, and he ordered the hit on Agnes' network. Siara knew information on Agnes' downline, it wasn't hard for her to find out who Agnes communicated with and work down the line."

So the badge in Agne's' hand hadn't been planted, she must have ripped it off the uniform of one of the officers.

"I don't believe it was Siara." She shook her head, trying to balance the information with the Siara she knew.

Kelvaras fished around in his pocket and pulled out two items. She studied them, without removing them from his hand. The first was a crest, a badge from a uniform.

"That doesn't prove anything," she said, pointing at the crest.

"Maybe this will." He pressed the button on the side of the communicator box. She clearly heard Siara's voice and another voice, distorted by distance, but when Siara called the person's name, she knew precisely who it was. A lump formed in her throat.

"The worst part is-" Kelvaras looked at her with such sympathy in his eyes.

"What?"

"Siara killed Agnes' herself."

"How do you know that?" Vyvica shot at him, she narrowed her eyes, feeling her heart race in her chest. She didn't want to hear the next bit of information.

He blinked slowly, obviously trying to decide the best way to tell her.

"She hasn't told me, if that's what you think. But there is information on this communicator that implicates her. She tells him that she's done the job."

"Has this got all of their conversations recorded on it?"

"As far as I can tell."

"How did you manage to come by it?"

"Vyvica, Siara isn't as straight-laced as you might think. She's drinking heavily and into some very strange drugs. She is comatose for most of the day and a good majority of the night. It isn't hard to search her apartment when she's out of it. Which brings me to another point. That place is bugged, I found at least three in the main room itself. I'm presuming that you aren't in the practice of bugging your own networks."

Ice ran down her spine, freezing her from the inside out. She put her head in her hands, her eyes stinging as she blinked rapidly to stop the tears from falling. All this time she thought that Siara had been a friend. She remembered back over the years they'd known each other. The person that he described didn't sound like the Siara she knew. An icy chill froze her face, even though they sat inside the warm café. His forehead creased as he scrutinised her.

"Are you all right?"

A rush of fury took over. Rage at him for telling her of her friend's betrayal, but worst of all, anger, pain and hurt at the loss of another friend.

Pushing herself up, her chair fell back with a metallic clunk. She shoved the table away with too much force. Kelvaras grabbed at his mug but hers smashed to the ground spraying coffee over other patrons. Complaints rang in her ears as she took off, running back to the apartment.

"Vyvica!"

Scrubbing tears from her eyes as she ran; she used her physical strength to fuel her screaming muscles. She reached the door, realising that she didn't have a key.

"Siara! Open up!" She pounded on the door. Up and down the corridor neighbours came out of their apartments to see what the commotion was about, but she didn't care.

"Siara, get your sorry arse out here!" A hand touched her shoulder; she turned and punched Kelvaras in the face. He stumbled backwards as the door cracked opened.

Vyvica put all her force behind her shoulder as she barged at the door and snapped the metal and wood frame. A terrified shriek echoed from the other side of the door as Vyvica stumbled into the room.

"What were you thinking?" Vyvica didn't recognise her own voice as she shouted at the pale-faced woman who stood before her.

"What are you talking about?" Siara knuckled her eyes, trying to clear them and wake up enough, but Vyvica wasn't prepared to wait. Growling, she launched herself and both stumbled over the back of the couch, and somersaulted onto the floor.

"You killed Agnes." Vyvica pulled her arm back and punched Siara in the face. Her knuckles stung on impact, probably split open.

Vyvica heard screaming and hands grasped at her, but she could only see her anger in a blinding redness around her.

"Agnes wasn't worth your friendship! She was a nerd, too nice, not like us. We've suffered in life, we understand hardship, she didn't!" Siara yelled back, kicking out at Vyvica savagely, connecting with her stomach.

Vyvica bent double, near vomiting, pausing long enough for Siara to crawl out from underneath her.

"Vyvica!" Kelvaras yelled. She felt a burning sensation across her bicep as she twisted towards him. Ignoring the pain, Vyvica spun around, her fist flying out and connecting. She spun once more, her foot hitting something solid and Siara crashed into the coffee table, splintering it. She bent down and launched punches at Siara again. Fingernails clawed at her face, leaving streaks of pain. Fists and feet blurred as they threw punches and kicks at each other.

They traded blows for some time, Vyvica was unsure how long, because time blurred. Next thing she remembered, she' was sitting, panting on the floor; the apartment in chaos around her.

Just what had she done?

Nothing moved around her, and the silence sat ominously in the room.

A hand touch her shoulder, tenderly. Without thinking, she grabbed and pulled it over her shoulder.

"It's me, Vyvica," Kelvaras said from his back, on the floor in front of her.

"That's Commander to you," she snapped, looking at Kelvaras as he lay crumpled on the ground amidst rumpled throws and cushions from the chair and couch. A throw was heaped up over a lump on the floor.

An immoveable form.

The splintered coffee table and a couple of pot plants were smashed.

"Where's Siara?" she growled. Kelvaras pushed himself upright and pointed at the object under the throw.

The breath left her body as she crawled over to the still form on the ground. She pulled back the cover and looked at a large bruise forming on the cheek and forehead of her friend.

"Oh..." Vyvica whimpered. She reached out a hand towards Siara. Pale hair covered her blood splattered face and her chest wasn't rising or falling.

Vyvica cautiously felt for a pulse.

Her hand slumped down by her side and her head dropped forward.

"What have I done?" she whispered, shaking her head.

"Hon', it's okay." She barely heard him, but an arm circled around her shoulders.

"No. I've killed my best friend!"

"Hon'..."

She shrugged him off. "Stop calling me that!"

Kelvaras moved around in front of her, but she refused to lift her eyes off the body that had been a close friend. Well, a friend anyway. She couldn't help but stare at the bruising on Siara's face; her nose sat on a strange angle, and seemed shorter. She remembered hearing a crunch and something gristly move under her hand as she threw punches.

"Siara?" She pushed at an arm. "Come on, Siara, wake up!" Her actions became frantic as she pushed her friend viciously; hoping the motion would restart her heart, get her breathing again.

"Vyvica!" From somewhere far away, someone called her name.

Sharp pain flared across her face and she looked around the room.

Kelvaras leaned in front of her, one hand on her shoulder, the other one waving in the air, trying to cool her face. She raised a hand to her cheek and the heat from the slap. She looked up at him, horror filling her.

"What the hell have I done?"

Siara is dead. I killed her, echoed around inside her head. A watery sob shook her body.

"Vyvica, she came at you like a hellcat, if you hadn't killed her, she would have killed you."

"I... I..." But words wouldn't form.

"Come on, we need to get you out of here before the authorities arrive. The neighbours would've called them by now."

"Huh?" She felt her body go limp. None of her limbs would respond. She tried to push herself to her feet, but she couldn't get up. Kelvaras placed his arm around her, lifting her. She looked at the body on the floor, noticing for the first time a knife in Siara's hand. She hadn't seen that when they had been fighting. She tentatively put her left hand to her right bicep and felt stickiness. She pulled her hand away, dumbfounded by her own blood.

A siren wailed, getting closer, breaking Vyvica from her stupor.

"Come on, Vyvica, we have to move." He hefted a shoulder under her arm and held her as upright as possible, moving her towards the door. He took her the opposite way along the landing, towards the rear of the building.

"Where're we going?"

"I know some of the shortcuts."

The screaming of the sirens got closer and her legs finally began to answer her brain's instructions. By the time they reached the back stairwell, she'd shrugged his arm away and could move on her own.

"Halt!" A computerised voice called out behind them.

Neither hesitated, both jumping to the landing below. A laser beam crashed into the railing above, crunching as it hit.

They ran, taking the steps two at a time before jumping to the next floor down. They scrambled out into the back alleyway, Vyvica stumbling over the paving. Kelvaras grabbed her arm to steady her as they heard another siren approaching and a tri-wheeled pod turned the corner. Both ran down the road, Kelvaras yelling instructions to Vyvica who was in the lead.

"Left!" She turned into a narrow alley. Vyvica ran as far as she could before coming to a dead end.

"What?" Vyvica turned around, puffing heavily as she glared at Kelvaras.

"Jump," he said, crouching down and springing up into the air. His hand reached out and latched onto the top of the top of the high chain fence and scrambled over with little difficulty. As Vyvica leapt up, scrambling with her legs to get purchase on the wire, a laser blast split the air between them. She hissed out an oath as strong arms pulled her from above, Kelvaras heaved her over the edge. She straddled the fence and saw the ledge he stood on. Towing her behind him, he started running along the narrow sill, as laser fire missed them. They ducked and weaved along the narrow precipice behind the wall of a building. A ladder led up onto the roof of the adjoining building, and he climbed quickly. Vyvica reached the top and found Kelvaras lying on the roof, breathing heavily.

"You all right?"

"Just... puffed..." He managed to mutter. She sat down with her back to the lip. Silence indicated no one in pursuit, but they couldn't afford to sit there and wait for the authorities to turn up either. She put her head between her knees and concentrated on slowing her breathing, her mouth dry, even in the cold outside air. Her clothing damp, she wiped sweat from her brow before it froze and blistered her skin.

A laser blast glancing off the precipice of the building galvanised them both into action. Kelvaras ran to the other side and looked down. An escape ladder led to an empty alleyway. He threw himself at it, swinging his feet over the edge and hooking them to the outside of the ladder, letting him slide down. He watched as Vyvica scrambled down, two rungs at a time, jumping the last bit to land beside him.

The alleyway headed straight into the heart of the city. There were no authorities at the opposite end of the alley.

"We'll run up this way, the authorities will assume we're heading back into the city."

"Where are we going, if we aren't going into the City?"

"Down."

"Huh?"

"Just start running, the noise of our footsteps will lead the authorities this way."

"But if they aren't here, why are we running that way?"

"Just do it, Vyvica!" He didn't look behind him, and she had to follow him towards the city. It wasn't long before the authorities on the roof spotted them.

They turned a slight bend and Kelvaras picked up a drain grate. "Now for the down."

"You expect me to get in there?" Her voice echoed around the narrow passage. She clamped a hand over her own mouth, before mouthing 'sorry' to Kelvaras.

"We don't have time to debate this. It is in, or prison. Your choice." He lowered himself into the drain, not waiting for her response. Before he shifted the grate back into place, she squeezed in beside him.

Her boots squelched as they sank into the soft mud at the bottom and she shrank down, crouching, she was forced to press against him. He lowered the grate into place. In the gloom, a darker hole surrounded by mud showed where the water drained away, the trickling sound of water telling her it was doing its job.

It smelt funky, but being close to Kelvaras, she could smell his salty sweat pheromones, bringing crazy images into her brain of hot embraces, and heated kisses.

He'd saved her; had helped her escape from the authorities. Prevented her from completely losing it when she realised- she swallowed back the bile. She'd killed Siara.

Could she finally trust him?

Could she let her guard down with him?

She looked up at where his face. His was upturned to the grate, concentrating on the sounds above. Sensing her gaze, he looked down at her and smiled, a soft, sweet, sympathetic smile.

A smile she could get used to.

CHAPTER FOURTEEN

Kelvaras could feel her breath on his face and he hoped that his increased heartbeat would be accredited to running, and not the close proximity of her body. Her scent wafted over him, a mixture of sweat and the lavender soap she used, along with the sharp metallic smell of blood from her wound. Her hair was right under his nose, soft and silky, even in the darkness of the drain he could see the sheen of it. He yearned to touch it, caress it, but it wasn't the time or place.

A steady rumble of running feet entered the alleyway above them. Several footsteps landed on the grate of the drain, deafening them within the confined chamber. It went quiet very quickly, too quiet.

"We'll wait a couple of minutes," he whispered into Vyvica's ear. He felt her tremble beside him. "Are you cold?"

She shook her head, keeping her face away from his. Pressed close together he felt warm, and he didn't want to lose that warmth. He slowly counted off seconds in his head, waiting long enough for the authorities to have gone far enough not hear or notice them. He eased himself out of the cramped position and listened at the drain, trying to see if the alley was clear. He couldn't hear anything, so he tentatively lifted the grate to see clearly down the road.

Looking both ways, he checked and double checked, before straightening and easing himself out of the confined space. He held a hand down to Vyvica. She surprised him by accepting and allowing him to pull her up. He was rewarded with a brilliant smile and a hushed thank you. She looked down at the ground, seemingly unable to look him in the eye. Obviously being pressed together, she'd been as affected by the closeness as he had. He grinned as he replaced the grate, and listening carefully, they both jogged back to the end of the street that led to the pod park.

He hoped that he'd tricked the authorities, at least long enough for them to escape but he couldn't guarantee they would fall for it.

They reached the end of the alleyway, and crossed over the street, keeping to the shadows as they edged their way to the threshold of the City. With sirens wailing, shops were shutting, and apartments locked down until the all clear siren sounded. There would be no way they could enter another building.

They came to the intersection of the main street. Opposite was the pod park, strangely not heavily guarded.

"What do you think?"

"Looks like a trap to me."

"Couldn't agree more. Two guards? Gate open? Too inviting."

"What should we do?"

Kelvaras shrugged. "I guess we wait and see."

Vyvica was quiet for a moment, deep in thought.

"Do they know who they are looking for?"

Kelvaras stared at her, wondering where her line of thought was going. "I don't know. What're you thinking?"

"We might be able to just walk out of here." He followed her gaze to the gate way.

"I don't get what you mean?"

"Our cards, they're false identities. If they don't know who they're looking for, we might be able to just walk."

He snorted. "And they might arrest us on the spot because we are the only ones trying to get into the pod park."

"Yes. I suppose you're right." She sounded disappointed,

"We could try it though."

"It is our only way out of here."

"We have the Intercity Transportation System." Kelvaras replied, well aware that it would upset Vyvica.

Vyvica glared at him.

"I'm just pointing out options," he replied. "But you're right. If we can't get on the pod, we're stuck here."

Vyvica nodded, and he hoped that she knew what she was doing, because he didn't have a clue.

CHAPTER FIFTEEN

Vyvica crouched beside Kelvaras as they surveyed the guards and the gate, his scent still thick in her nostrils; leather and sweat. Her body warmed as she thought about the closeness they had been forced into in the drain. The feeling just wouldn't leave her.

"I propose we walk up to them, and at the last minute, we run to the gates," Kelvaras said.

"Too risky, we need to disarm them. And I think I know how." Vyvica smiled at him.

"How?"

Vyvica stood up, pushed her hood off, and fluffed up her hair. She shook it until it fell down her back, before sauntering out from the corner. She heard Kelvaras hiss something to her, but she ignored him.

Her hips swayed as she walked up to the guards, both moving together and shifting their guns.

"Afternoon boys."

"Identification, please."

Vyvica put a hand down the front of her jacket, but couldn't reach, so she unzipped her jacket, showing off more cleavage. She didn't know what kind of effect it would have on them, but it normally worked. She found her card and handed it over. One took the card and inserted it into the reader. He looked up from the reader at Vyvica, but she couldn't see his expression behind the visor.

The second one lowered his gun and trained it on her. Her heart threatened to leap out of her throat, but she remained calm on the outside.

"Problem?" She smiled and lowered her head so she was looking at them from under her eyelashes.

The first guard lowered the reader to show a red flashing light.

"We're shutting down the city. We can't allow you to leave."

"Oh, come on guys, I really need to get out of here." She pouted. Seeing that it wasn't going to work, she decided on another course of action.

Before the second guard could react, she grabbed the gun and pushed it up. He pulled on the trigger, and a stream of laser blasted onto the building behind Vyvica. Using the surprise, she kicked the first guard in the stomach and kneed the second guard in the groin.

"Run!" Kelvaras shouted at her as he rounded the corner. Plasma streams erupted above her head and she ducked as she took off, heading towards the gate. Laser blasts showered them in sparks and debris. Vyvica weaved and dived, pounding steps and heavy panting behind her, she hoped it was Kelvaras.

She saw the gate sliding closed and swore.

"Damn, damn, damn, damn"," she muttered, but didn't slow down. An arm encircled her shoulders, pulling her to the left to slip between the closing gate and the gatepost. They stumbled and fell as they landed inside the gate, a puff of wind hitting her face as the gate slammed shut.

Kelvaras dragged her to her feet as he ran across the yard to the pod. Laser blasts created showers of ice and snow around their feet as they ran. Vyvica punched the door button as she slammed into the side of the pod. The door incrementally opened, and while still halfway, she leapt up and swung her legs into the craft. Kelvaras jumped up after her, and she hit the raise button as he scrambled onto the slope. The upwards movement propelled him into the ship, and he somersaulted to his feet as she fired up the engine.

She pushed the boosters hard, the pod responding and boosting them into the air, using the momentum to fire the rockets. They cleared the top of the security fence, lasers firing all around them. The pod sped away, the machine accelerating to its limits.

CHAPTER SIXTEEN

Kelvaras sat in the co-pilot's seat, watching her. Vyvica continued to monitor the screens flickering on the panel as they moved further away from Marr. There was still the chance that they would be followed and fired upon, but the further away they got, the more relaxed her shoulders got.

She seemed to run on autopilot, methodically checking all the gauges and dials on the control panel, even though they were mid-flight.

"Commander?" he asked tentatively.

"Mmmm."

"Are you alright?"

She closed her eyes, tightly, before opening them again. She didn't turn to look at him, but he could see tears glistening on her lashes.

"Hey, I don't want you to get all teary-eyed on me." This made her turn and glare at him.

"I'm not going to cry." Her eyes were glassy.

"But you do need to talk about what happened back there. You scared the hell out of me."

She raised an eyebrow, almost amused. "Nothing happened."

"You call that nothing? You can't bury it and hope it doesn't come back up."

"I'm not burying it. I killed my best friend..." She paused, closed her eyes again, took a deep breath, and stared straight at him. Her eyes were no longer shiny, and they held his gaze.

"Yeah," Kelvaras encouraged her.

"I have to accept the consequences."

"Consequences? It was self-defence!"

"Was it? I attacked her first."

"Oh, for goodness sake. The woman was informing on you. Yes, you struck first. Would you rather do that? Or be stabbed in the back?

Vyvica ducked her head, her cheeks flushing, she rubbed at her upper arm where the blood had dried on her jacket. "My anger overtook me."

"Yeah, and it's spectacular. Remind me to never piss you off again."

She chuckled, a genuine laugh. The sound surprised him and it changed her whole face, her eyes twinkling with delight.

"She also had a weapon, you didn't."

Vyvica looked away, deep in thought. Getting up from his seat, he reached over and touched her shoulder, careful to avoid the wound, leaving his hand there. Looking up at him, she sighed a little, it was too much for him and he pulled her into his arms.

And she allowed him.

Her body, tucked in next to his, felt divine. Heat radiated off her, and his body soaked it up. Resting her head on his chest, he hoped she couldn't tell that his heart beat had trebled. Lifting her chin, he leaned down and brushed his lips over hers. Vyvica didn't jerk away or resist, so he deepened the kiss.

She moaned a little as he licked across her bottom lip. She sighed as she opened her mouth, her tongue flicking out to connect with his. Her taste, her scent filled his nose, and he couldn't resist, his other hand reached down and pushed up underneath her jacket.

She pulled away, her eyes turning from liquid to ice. Closing her eyes, she lounged back in her seat, swinging her feet up onto the rest.

She'd shut him down. Deciding to take what he'd been given, and not push his luck, Kelvaras sat back on his own seat and contemplated the incident in Marr.

With the drug concoction she had been on, Siara had been dangerous. It would've only been a matter of time before she brought down the D'Authian Guards. Vyvica had eliminated the problem very quickly and efficiently. With such efficiency it frightened him. Her moves were lightning fast and lethal.

But the fact Siara worked for Ch'ar had been the biggest problem for them.

Them.

Since when had he thought himself part of the D'Authian Guards?

He worked for Ch'ar too.

Both were paying him.

Where did his loyalty lie?

D'Authian Guards were paying him to find the leak. He had.

Now, he had to find a way to get them back to the Crown City in order to collect Ch'ar's pay.

Something inside him stirred. He wished he could tell Vyvica why he was really there, but she would probably kill him on the spot.

Not *probably*, she'd definitely kill him.

The D'Authian Guard were the worthier cause, he had to acknowledge that. They wanted their planet back to run it the way it had been for centuries.

Ch'ar was only in it for the mineral resources and for political gain.

Kelvaras' throat thickened and his chest tightened. He'd buried his conscience a long time ago. He went with the highest bidder, money won over conscience every time. How could he survive as a vigilante if he thought too much about how his actions would affect those around him?

Yet here he was, contemplating his role.

The money he earned went to a good cause; he gave it to his mum to help her raise his older, intellectually-handicapped sister and others like her. His mother had successfully kept them hidden from the authorities in secret underground facilities. Kelvaras loved and respected his sister, but the idea of her being taken away to an institution, or incarcerated in a prison for the mentally incapable...he shook his head. Helping his mother was the only way he could assist. It was too dangerous for him to return, so he hadn't seen his mother or sister for several years, not since he embarked on his vocation. Not that he'd originally chosen it, but the military training had helped.

"Did Siara say anything to you about Agnes?" Vyvica's voice sounded hollow.

"Pardon?"

"Did Siara say anything about Agnes?"

"She didn't say a lot about her, but when she did, it wasn't nice."

"Oh."

"Siara was a liability to the organisation. You know that, don't you?"

"I guess. I can't get over how jealous she was of Agnes. Agnes wouldn't have hurt anyone, she was considerate and kind. The opposite of Siara."

"I think anyone would be the opposite of Siara. She was taking some nasty things, and when she flew into a rage, it wasn't nice. It scared me to watch the two of you fight. You were so evenly matched."

"You certainly weren't going to step in."

"And have my head smashed open? I don't think so." He smiled, but Vyvica's face remained icy.

"Siara and Agnes helped me when we first arrived at Apos. I was so distraught at having to leave my father behind. I don't know if he's still alive or not. But he's the only family I have. Agnes was kind and listened to me while I spoke for hours about him. Siara was the one that got me back into physical training. They both helped me in their own way."

"I'm sorry for your loss, Vyvica."

Vyvica turned to look at him, a strange look in her eye.

"Thank you." Her reply was genuine and earnest. "I've no one left," she said sadly.

Kelvaras didn't know what to say. If they'd left him behind, her father was as good as dead.

"What about Tyron?" he asked. He hadn't worked that one out yet.

She laughed again. "Tyron and I have an unusual relationship. Probably more like father and daughter.

He's been in active service longer than I have, and he is full of good knowledge."

"So you two aren't..."

She turned sharply to look at him. "Hell, no!" Her vehemence was strong. "Why do you ask?"

He let out his breath, unaware he had been holding it, and laughed. "I was just wondering. The way he treats you, I thought you two were...you know...maybe a couple."

"Goodness, no! I would probably have killed him by now."

Kelvaras chuckled.

He could imagine it.

CHAPTER SEVENTEEN

In the Ops Room, Vyvica sat at the table, head down, looking at her tightly clasped hands. Tyron sat quietly, digesting all the information she'd told him, with interjections from Kelvaras.

Her stomach churned every time she thought of what she'd done. Killing someone who wasn't the enemy was new for her. She'd had a sleepless night, and couldn't make eye contact with Tyron. She might be the commander of the outfit, but she still needed to account for her actions and face the consequences.

"And you're certain that she was the mole?" Tyron directed the question to Kelvaras, who sat on the opposite side of the room. She looked up at him, hoping that he would make her feel justified.

"Siara had a communicator with a direct link to Ch'ar."

"And you know this...how?" Tyron narrowed his eyes. The interrogation was about to begin in earnest.

Kelvaras placed the communicator on the table. Tyron looked at it, then back up to Kelvaras, waiting on his explanation.

"Conversations are recorded on it."

"I thought conversations weren't recorded on such devices."

"Generally they aren't, but this device can. And it was activated by the other party, Siara had no idea that her conversations were being recorded. It isn't hard to record discussions if you have the right tools and information," Kelvaras said.

Vyvica felt her scalp itch at the insinuated insult.

"And what information were you able to find out?" Tyron pressed.

"That she and Ch'ar were passing information to each other."

"And how could you tell this?"

"If you listen to it, you'll know. Also the satellite address of the caller."

"You know Ch'ar's satellite address?"

"No, but the originating signal is from the Crown City of Althu."

Tyron turned to look at Vyvica. Worry pulled a notch between his eyebrows. The affection in his look eased her curdling stomach.

"Anything else you can tell us?" she asked.

"Siara gave him exact information and from what I could gather, she only passed some of it through to you.

"She also spent a lot of time with a gentleman—a term I use rather loosely—by the name of Stott Forthright. He's the head of the local gang of Marr, in fact his family were one of the prime instigators of building the city.

"He provided her with drugs and alcohol, most of the stuff confiscated when it first arrives into the city. Siara was pretty much off her face most of the time. She made an effort the first day I was with her, but by the third day she needed her daily fix on a regular basis."

"Stott Forthright? He is head of the Neem Cartel and quite tight with Ch'ar," Tyron said. The more Tyron and Kelvaras talked, the more Vyvica's hands sweated. She wiped them on her pants, letting their voices wash over her.

Information from their network had been deliberately passed onto Ch'ar, but why hadn't he taken her out?

How had she not figured this out?

Why had they been so blind?

"Would Forthright have introduced Siara to Ch'ar?" Vyvica asked.

"From what I learnt, Ch'ar put Siara and Forthright in touch with each other." Kelvaras said.

Tyron whistled loudly. "That's bad," he said, shaking his head, obviously feeling as deceived as Vyvica.

"How long?"

"I don't know."

"How did you manage to find this information out?"

"When she was out of her head, she'd tell you anything and not remember."

"How reliable is the information?" Vyvica asked, watching Kelvaras' gaze harden and his jaw move as he clenched his teeth.

"It's all that I have. You can believe me if you want to, you're paying me, remember?"

Conflicting thoughts raced through her mind. Could Siara have made this up to make herself look more attractive to Kelvaras?

"Did anything happen between you and Siara?" Vyvica asked, his anger raising her own ire. Tyron turned to stare at her, she caught the movement in her peripheral vision, but remained focused on Kelvaras'.

Kelvaras grimaced. "A gentleman never tells."

Vyvica stood up quickly, Kelvaras stood at the same instant, and readied himself for her to attack him.

She tried not to let the tears show as she turned and left the room.

CHAPTER EIGHTEEN

Landing heavily on her back, Vyvica panted with anger, frustration and exhaustion. She'd been in the training room for an hour, trying to relieve the tension that weighed on her shoulders.

Guilt was the prime instigator, and physical activity was one way to remove it.

She waited, catching her breath. She'd been tackling the assault course. Not focusing on the task, she'd slipped, falling from the rope and landing on the padding.

A stupid mistake.

She got up, gingerly, nothing broken, a small strain in her side from where the rope caught her on the way down. She walked to the control panel and wiped the room.

Grabbing her towel and sipping water, she opened the door to leave, but thought better of it.

She went back to the panel.

"Alex? That simulation sorted yet?" She waited by the comms for his response.

"Yeah, Commander. You want the new one up now?"

"Yes please, Alex." She returned to the bench, wiped sweat from her face and took another deep mouthful of water. The coolness washed down her throat and reached her stomach.

"You only have to call out to end the simulation, OK?"

Vyvica ignored him.

A flicker of light concentrated in the centre of the room and three men materialised.

"Good afternoon gentleman," she called out. They turned towards her as she dropped her towel and bottle onto the bench, and sauntered into the middle of the room.

"Are we ready to rock?"

No response, but she hadn't expected one. She took a step backwards and poised herself, one arm raised at head height, the other drawn back behind her. The muscles across her shoulders stretched and her thighs flexed as she squatted.

This was what she needed.

"Come and get it," she whispered. All three came at her at once, surprising her. She kept an eye on all of them, her neck twisting around as they circled her. The one out of her vision struck first, hitting her in the small of her back with his foot. Grunting, she fell forward, stumbling onto her knees. She saw the punch coming, aimed at her head and ducked, using the momentum of her body to roll sideways. Landing firmly on her feet, she twisted around, moving in front of the men.

They sized her up again before they lined up and charged.

Unsure who to hit first, Vyvica jumped into the air, swinging her legs out sidewise from her body while she punched downwards.

She didn't expect to be pulled from the air.

Crashing hard, the wind knocked out of her. One simulant sat on her chest, while a second punched her in the face.

Dazed and confused, she tried to twist around, but the one sitting on her pinned her with his weight and no matter what she tried, she couldn't budge him.

Her vision blurred and she cried out with the stinging pain across her cheekbone.

She dug down deep within, took as deep a breath as she could and centred her guilt, allowing her frustration to grow from it. She yelled out, emptying her lungs. Bucking her body to raise her knees, she pushed up and arched her back.

The man sitting on her slid off and she continued the backward somersault, kicking out, connecting with the small of her assailant's back. He fell forward, and she landed on her feet astride him, punching down towards his kidney and aiming her second fist to a spot at the base of his skull. She felt a satisfying crack under her knuckles.

She spun around on her left leg, her right leg pulled into her chest. She rotated out, her foot connecting with the stomach of the second simulant, but strong hands gripped her from behind, pulling her arms awkwardly behind her.

The other attacker came in, pummelling her stomach and face with renewed aggression.

Tears burned the cuts on her cheeks, her nose clogged with blood and mucus, but she still refused to stop the simulation.

She needed this.

Punishment for killing a friend.

It would remove the burden of guilt she carried.

The grip on her arms lessened and she collapsed sobbing onto the ground. Hands reached out, but through the haze she brushed them away, half-heartedly defending herself.

"Vyvica, it's me." Kelvaras' soft voice penetrated through the fog of self-pity.

She wiped away the tears and saw Kelvaras kneeling down beside her. He held her towel and bottle. She took the bottle from him, allowing him to see her tears.

"Are you okay?" he asked. She looked at the concern in his eyes, the colour deep and dark, neither condemning nor judging her. She wrapped her arms around him, her face buried in his neck, her body shaking from the sobs. Kelvaras sat down beside her, pulling her onto his lap, allowing her to cry.

"Is this about Siara?"

She continued to sob, unable to stop. It wasn't just Siara, it was Agnes as well, and all those they had lost that night when they lost Althu. Years of pushing everything down and suppressing it bubbled to the surface from a deep well of hurt. She cried until she couldn't cry anymore, feeling safe and secure in the arms of the one man who might actually understand.

"How do you cope?" she said.

"With what?"

"Everything. Death. Friendship. How do you juggle all those things and make them fit together into your life?"

Kelvaras sighed. She sat up and looked at him. He held one of her hands, his fingers playing over the top of her knuckles, leaving pleasant tingling feelings within her body.

"I guess I'm just a man, we compartmentalise everything. Women are unique in that everything is connected, your friendships and deaths are interconnected. Your job and friendships are also. Whereas us men, we only deal with one thing at a time. I dealt with Siara on a day to day basis. Her death was shocking, yes, but it happened, and you can't undo it."

"How am I supposed to cope? I'm supposed to be the leader of this group, yet I can't lead them with men like Tyron and the Council wanting to know my every step. I want to get back into the City. I want to find my father. We've waited long enough. Why doesn't the Council have a plan yet?"

"From what I understand, the Council is very close to having a plan."

"But it will take another five years to implement it."

"What's wrong with that?"

Vyvica's breath froze in her throat and she snatched her hand free from Kelvaras' fingers. "What's wrong with that? I'll tell you. We left my father in that City to try and negotiate. I didn't want to leave him, but I had to. I want to free my father and get rid of Ch'ar once and for all."

"Vyvica, the Council knows what's best, and they are thinking about the greater good for the group.

Tyron said that they are the ones that make the big decisions."

"The greater good? The only thing they are concerned about is not looking bad in front of the Federation. I'm almost beginning to suspect that the Council are in on it with Ch'ar." She pushed herself onto her knees, ready to get up and move away.

"That's an extreme comment to make. That sounds like treason to me."

"Treason? You think I'm worried about treason? All I want is my father back."

She snatched the bottle from him, as he brought the towel up to her face.

"Leave it." She growled.

"I'm only trying to help. And what were you trying to do in here? Get yourself killed?"

"Simulations can't kill."

"They seemed to be doing a bloody good job of not killing you." Sarcasm deepened his voice. "What were you thinking?"

"I needed the exercise."

"There is a big line between exercise and punishment."

She took a mouthful of water. Her left eye swelling, and tentatively reached a hand to touch it. A large cut bled through her eyebrow, and she took the towel from him, pressing it to stem the flow.

"Let's get you to the medic."

"Don't touch me," she said through gritted teeth.

"Vyvica," he pleaded. But he backed off as she glared at him with her one good eye. Anger resonated through her soul. The guilt gone, anger now filled its place.

"Will you stop addressing me by that name? I'm the commander."

"Vyvica is your given name."

"And I only allow those who are friends to use it."

"Come on, after all we have been through together"?"

"Whose side are you on? Mine or Tyron's?"

Kelvaras paled and rocked back on his heels.

"I'm working for the D'Authian Guards, *Commander*." He got to his feet, saluted and left the room.

Fresh tears rolled down her cheeks. She hadn't asked for Kelvaras to enter her life, but he had gotten under her skin.

For now.

CHAPTER NINETEEN

Kelvaras ground his teeth as he marched out of the training room.

How could she be so stubborn? Those simulants were really beating her up, and for what? Why had she inflicted that on herself? Anger? Frustration? Guilt?

His heart had leapt out of his chest when he had seen her lying on the floor like that. The pummelling she took had frightened him, and she lay there, trembling. And then she'd hugged him, he relaxed as he thought how nice it was to comfort someone, to comfort her. How had the conversation gotten out of control? He'd only suggested that the Council were doing their job. Was she so opposed to the Council? She wouldn't be the commander if she did. Only royalty were higher than the Council...

He found himself heading to the ops room. Tyron wasn't there, so he continued onto the Command Room. He pressed the intercom.

"Yes?"

"It's Kelvaras Mason, is Tyron there?"

"No, Tyron is in his quarters."

"Can you tell me where his quarters are?"

"He advised that he didn't want to be disturbed."

"I need to speak with him urgently. Tell him I'll meet him in the ops room." He stalked off without waiting for a response. He didn't want to run into Vyvica coming out of the training room or in the Ops Room. Pressing the button to open the door, he cautiously peered in. The room lay empty. He entered, closing the door behind him.

Leaning against it, he tried to recapture his fractured thoughts.

Vyvica.

She made him angry.

Really angry.

She had no right to endanger herself so mindlessly, and for what?

Because she had feelings? Women were allowed to feel, but not Vyvica? Why was she so special that she couldn't accept her own emotions?

Oh no, Vyvica wasn't allowed to act like a lady, be treated like a lady or even speak like a lady. She wanted to be treated like a man, in a man's position.

The only thing ladylike about her, was her impatience to get things done.

Taking a deep breath, he sat in the chair opposite the door, propping his feet up on the table, but his frayed nerves left him restless. He swung his feet to the floor and went to the large window which looked out over the mechanics bay.

He watched a couple of mechanics having a heated discussion, another intervened and they all dispersed in different directions. No sound of metal on metal or the smell of welding gases permeated the room. The triple glazing cut out all sound and kept the room warm. The door opened and Vyvica entered.

His heart skipped a beat as he took in her appearance. She'd come directly from the Training room, her singlet top blood-stained, one eye bright red and swollen shut. She looked up and stepped back when she saw him standing at the window.

"What're you doing here?"

"Waiting on Tyron," he said, injecting coolness and efficiency into his voice. Vyvica nodded and proceeded to the ice unit where she pulled a bag of slush from the front panel and applied it to her cheek and eyebrow as she sat, tipping her head back.

Kelvaras could see the pulse in her throat and he fought the overwhelming desire to kiss that throbbing point. It took considerable control to turn his back to her.

His throat tightened, and pain twisted in his chest. He closed his eyes. He couldn't afford to fall for Vyvica, she was too selfish. In a tight situation she wouldn't be relied upon to work with the team.

A shower of sparks caught his attention and he used the distraction to temper his thoughts.

The door whooshed opened and Tyron entered and nodded to Kelvaras. He looked at Vyvica and raised an eyebrow to Kelvaras, who shrugged his response.

"Do you want some privacy?" Vyvica asked. Her voice cold, her good eye closed.

"We'll leave you to it," Tyron said, indicating for Kelvaras to follow him.

"I don't think there's anything he'll tell you that can't be shared with me."

Kelvaras stopped as Tyron turned back towards her.

"What are you talking about? And while you're talking, would you mind telling me who did this to you? It certainly wasn't Kelvaras, which surprises me."

"I had Alex work up the simulation," she said. Tyron smirked.

At least he could see the humour in the situation, Kelvaras thought.

"He must have geared it up a hell of a lot." Tyron suggested as he lifted the icepack from her mutilated face.

"He did exactly as I asked him. At least he listens when I issue commands." Her pointed glance fell on Kelvaras, who smiled.

"I had to halt the simulation; she was getting quite a beating," Kelvaras stated.

"How dare you! I would've got myself out of the situation."

"Really? When?" Kelvaras challenged.

"When I was ready."

"You wouldn't have been able to halt it if you were unconscious."

She didn't respond, but her jaw worked as she ground her teeth.

"Times up, couldn't think of anything to say fast enough, I win," Kelvaras said.

Tyron looked between the two of them.

"I have to say that that was the most stupid thing I have ever seen, and I have seen some dumb things. Vyvica, you are the head of the King's own bodyguard. Act like it." Kelvaras snapped.

"Act like it? How dare you, how else am I to get training?"

"You call that training?" Tyron pointed to her face.

Her skin flushed to match the redness that the icepack had put on half of her face. But she pressed her lips into a slit. The tension in the room built to straining point.

"I'm in prime physical condition..."

"Physical condition does not win wars. Having nous and mental stamina does. Get that into your thick-"

"Enough!" Tyron stepped between them his face contorted and red, but Vyvica stood up, facing off with Kelvaras.

"Thick what? I'll have you know-"

Kelvaras turned his back on her and paced away. Without warning, Vyvica flew across the table at him, but he heard her and was ready. Grabbing her arm and using her forward motion, he spun around bringing her with him, pinning her arm up her back with one hand, and holding her neck at a strange angle. Her body was hard against his and she couldn't move.

"That wasn't smart now, was it?" The heat from her body singed his skin. "Another example of how you act first and think afterwards."

His heart rate increased as he held her close. He could smell her scent, intoxicating and sensual. His pulse raced with excitement.

She wriggled in his grasp before she attempted to grate her foot down his instep, but he kicked her foot out and twisted the other one away from her. Her whole balance now rested on his hip. If she lifted her other leg, she wouldn't be able to get any purchase or kick out with any intensity.

A gurgle of anger erupted from her throat.

That guttural sound ripped at his heart.

He wanted to spin her around and kiss her, taste her, feel her heat beneath his own body.

His body ached with want. If only she would calm down. He hadn't tried to upset her.

He looked down and saw her chest heaving with anger. Her top pulled away from her shoulder to reveal a mark like a stylised rose on her back.

"What's that?" he asked, looking up at Tyron.

"What?" Tyron and Vyvica asked at the same time. Vyvica's breath hitched in her throat. She looked up, eyes widened, and expression shocked.

"It's just a beauty mark."

"A beauty mark? It looks more like a tattoo."

"No, it's a beauty mark. Now let me go," she said, her face growing pale.

"Let her go." Tyron growled. Kelvaras had never heard that tone before. It was one that meant follow his orders...or else.

He released her and she slumped to the floor.

"Use your head, *Commander.* Stop acting on impulse."

Tyron came around the table and helped her to her feet, but she refused his assistance. She slowly raised herself to her feet.

"Your job here is done, Mason. Pack your bags and leave." She pushed past Tyron, pain and emotion warring across her face and through her body as she stalked from the room.

Tyron glared at Kelvaras.

"She had it coming. Don't blame me, I'm not here to play 'pin the blame on the vigilante'. I did my job, I found your problem."

"You did, but you didn't need to humiliate her in the process."

"Humiliate her? It's about time someone threw the ice queen off her pinnacle. She comes across as having everything under control, but she doesn't. She got hammered in the training room because she was trying to get rid of her guilt. She isn't perfect."

Tyron's shoulders relaxed and he blew out a breath. "No one said she was," Tyron said quietly. He slumped into a chair, ducking his head down. His shoulders were shaking and Kelvaras looked at the second in command. Were they all falling to pieces? He pulled a hand through his hair as he contemplated his next move.

He looked back at Tyron when he heard the older man take a breath. Tyron threw back his head and laughed.

"It was actually worth it to see the look on her face when you had her pinned against you; the absolute hatred. Man, if you could've seen her, she would've killed you with that look."

"Don't worry, I don't think I'll be hanging around much, I actually value my life."

CHAPTER TWENTY

Tears wet Vyvica's face as she sat slumped at the door of her quarters.

How dare he humiliate me like that!

He'd held her arm behind her back, her opposite arm pulled across her chest. The restricted movement had frightened her. When she'd tried to kick him, he'd countered so fast.

Never before had she felt so vulnerable.

In the training room, they'd had a moment, where she let her guard down, and it had felt so nice...lovely. Electric tingles radiated across her skin as she remembered his touch.

But he was completely different in the Ops Room. The complete opposite; cold, calculating. His words had hurt.

She didn't feel anger or guilt anymore, just...empty.

She pushed the wetness from her face, stood up and looked into the image reflector. A puffy, red eye and a swollen, blackening eye stared back at her, not a good look for the commander. Huffing a sigh, she turned on her shower unit, and stepped under the hot waves of steam. It permeated through her long hair, blew over her face. Droplets condensed on her body and ran down her curves. She didn't wash, just stood under the steam, allowing herself to think. She loved to shower for that purpose, something to do with negative ions in the water particles.

Her best ideas always came whilst in the shower, and a plan was definitely formulating.

She needed to get back to the Crown City.

This war had been going on long enough, and she needed it to stop.

No one else could do it.

She turned the nozzle off and wrapped a towel around herself.

She dressed in her white tank top and pale camo pants, her warm over-jacket tightly buckled at her waist.

Her professional look.

She took a steadying breath and used the communicator to summon Tyron. They needed to talk, without Kelvaras poking his nose in.

She needed to be taken seriously.

The humour in Tyron's face at the way Kelvaras had manhandled her annoyed her. Kelvaras had gotten under her skin.

That had to end.

The Ice Queen was back.

The landing resonated with the sound of her brisk march to the Ops Room. She hesitated outside the door, unsure if Kelvaras would still be inside. As it opened, she breathed a sigh of relief, entered the empty room and grabbed water from the ice unit. She flipped the cap off and let the ice cold liquid fill her mouth, taking away the dry cotton feeling. Compared to her hot shower, it sent a shot of clarity through her thoughts.

Tyron entered the room solemnly. She studied his face, expecting to see humour there, but he kept it composed. His eyes held a slight twinkle to them. Gritting her teeth, she proceeded. "I trust you've dealt with Kelvaras and sent him on his way."

"No, he still has some work to do."

Vyvica bristled. "What do you mean, more work? He found the leak."

"There could be more than one leak, Vyvica, we can't just walk away from it and not be totally sure we've resolved the problem." He clasped his hands in front of him, keeping his head down.

"Whose side are you on?" Vyvica narrowed her eyes.

"Pardon? What do you mean?" Tyron looked flustered for a moment.

"Do you support me, or Kelvaras?" she asked. The relieved look on his face worried her a little.

"You're the commander, Vyvica."

"You have an extremely funny way of showing it. You found it amusing that Kelvaras beat me before."

Tyron blushed at her comments and a hint of a smile pulled at his mouth.

"So much for being my bodyguard. You let him hold me there like that."

"I'm sorry, Commander. But, you-" He looked up at her, his gaze penetrating her own. "You deserved it, you've given him a hard time too." The humour now gone, Vyvica took a deep breath in.

Tyron was always frank with her.

And she didn't always appreciate it.

Like now.

But she knew he was right.

"He's a vigilante. He could've killed me. Then where would we be?"

"You're right." The contrite man stood before her. The sincerity on his face along with the flash of recognition of the situation she'd been in.

"I did tell him to let you go. But you both were acting very childish."

Vyvica glared at him.

"Sorry," he mumbled.

"That isn't what I called you in for." She paused, taking a sip of water, and started pacing across the room. "I think we need to start mobilising and hit the Crown City of Althu. We've been wasting time trying to gather intelligence. Most of it is false. We know what the inside of the castle looks like, we know where all the secret doorways and alcoves are. We need to strike now."

Tyron stroked his chin thoughtfully.

"Well?"

"Kelvaras suggested the same thing," Tyron replied.

"He did?" She couldn't keep the surprise and suspicion from her voice.

"He suggested that we had all of the information we needed. He pretty much put it like you did."

"And what's your opinion?"

"I think we need to make a watertight plan before we go charging off. We abandoned the place; no doubt there are new security measures."

She rolled her eyes. "We have the best in the business among our crew; surely someone will be able to disable any security that Ch'ar has put into place."

"Maybe, but we really don't need to be going off all gung-ho. We need to be thorough and methodical. The Council will need to know of the plans and approve of them."

Vyvica nodded. This stupid war had gone on long enough. All she wanted was to find her father.

"Tyron, I can't keep doing this. I need to put an end to this occupation." She sat and rested her head on her arms. She felt Tyron move into the seat next to her, and put an arm around her shoulder.

"I know, hon'." He braved her glare and smiled at her. "I've known you longer than you remember. It's hard not having your father around, he was a good man."

"He is a good man."

"We don't know that for sure. We have to hope that he's managed to keep his wits about him and he's still alive."

"I have to believe that Ch'ar needs him alive." Vyvica sighed. She turned to Tyron. "Why did no one make plans to go back in earlier, to rescue the king and regain the castle?"

"It wasn't that easy. When we left, the king had given us instructions to keep his daughter safe." He squeezed her shoulders and she nestled into him.

"It doesn't make sense. You would think that keeping him safe would have been the most important thing."

"When you have something as precious as a child, you will understand."

Vyvica pulled out of Tyron's embrace and smiled. "Thank you."

"What for?"

"Making it easier for me."

"That's my job Vyvica, to make sure that you're kept out of harm's way."

"And the best way to do that was to make me commander of the D'Authian Guard?"

"No, you earned that position on your own."

CHAPTER TWENTY-ONE

Vyvica's chest contracted as she thought about what she perceived as the Council's delaying tactics. After several days, they were still no closer to making a decision. So she made one.

She wanted her father back.

Vyvica couldn't wait for 'plans to fall into place' any longer. The pain threatened to crush her as she sat in the pilot's seat of her pod.

The delay hadn't garnered them any new information and it appeared that they'd wasted five years. While Tyron, Kelvaras and all of them plotted it out, she would make an attempt to get into the city and find out what had happened to her father.

While Tyron's little spiel had sounded good, it didn't put her at ease.

Why had they waited so long?

Sitting in her pod, moving over the snow fields, eleven hours after leaving the base, she knew she risked a lot. She hoped to land the pod close by and sneak into the castle, but that wasn't necessarily going to be easy. As Tyron had pointed out, security could've been changed, or tightened.

But then, would they necessarily know about the escape tunnels that she knew of? Tyron had shown her where most of them were when she was younger. She hadn't been sure why at the time, but was pleased he had.

Her device pounded instrumental music into her head. She needed inspiration. Her thoughts and memories of her father grew stronger as she sped through the frozen wasteland, heading north to the Crown City, her home city.

She closed her eyes, an image of her father flashed up, of him slamming the door in her face. It haunted her, the last vision she'd had of him, but now she understood why he had done it. He had been protecting her.

He loved her.

His act of abandonment was actually an act of love.

"I'm coming, Dad," she muttered.

Vyvica flew a mere metre above the ground, hoping to avoid radar detection. She'd packed her thermal gear as she would have to spend at least an hour in the elements, and the outside temperature was minus five on a good day.

For safety, she counted on the trek taking two hours, so packed a couple of drinks, her outside jacket and pants, ready for her own final assault.

She had her weapons, too. Hand to hand combat was her preference, but that really wouldn't be an option if there were more than three combatants, and her efforts a week ago, in which she'd been severely beaten by three simulants, had shaken her confidence. It had taken a few days for the bruising to fade, and she'd endured many strange looks from her fellow D'Authian Guards. Tyron had banned her from training on her own, and she hadn't had an opportunity to go back and try again.

She shivered as she drew closer, a signal repeatedly flashed on her control panel confirming that she was within a short distance of her dropoff point. Now she wished she'd told Tyron her plans, but she knew that he would've stopped her.

Her heart pounded as she thought about Kelvaras. He would've told Tyron, or come with her, or, he would've physically restrained her, and she didn't want that.

A frisson of excitement and sadness skimmed through her veins.

Her feelings were a jumbled mess. Yes, he'd humiliated her, but her body hummed to a new tune whenever she thought about him.

She didn't want to admit it but, damn it, she liked the guy...

A little more than liked...?

Vyvica couldn't say the word, her world was too complicated for a relationship. How could she remain loyal to her troops and be with a man at the same time? And she'd lost two close friends, and had the emotional torment to overcome before she could commit friendship to anyone else.

It could happen to Kelvaras too. He could die. It nearly killed me when Agnes died, it would if...

It was all too hard.

Instead of telling anyone, she'd snuck off.

The cave mouth opened up, wide and dark. The perfect spot for her to hide her pod while she entered the city. She set it down on the uneven frozen ground within, and used the boosters to ease her pod back as far as she could into the darkness. She hit the camouflage button, and the pod shimmered before turning a matt black. From a distance no one would know that a vessel sat concealed within the cave.

After the cooldown period, she donned her exterior gear, thick padded jacket, warm fleece lined pants, wet protection boots and thick fur lined gloves. Goggles protected her eyes from the severe cold as she prepared to head out of the vessel.

Her heart lurched with—excitement? Anticipation? Fear?

A surge of adrenaline moved her out of the pod, pulling the hood up on her jacket, and buckling it with the snood underneath her chin. Before she even left the pod, sweat formed on her forehead, but once she got outside she would quickly cool down. She grabbed her pack, took a deep breath of warm air and headed out.

A blast of cold air hit her as she opened the hatch. As predicted, it was cold, a lot colder than she'd anticipated, but once she got moving, the thermo gear would regulate her body temperature.

She checked the positioning device. North, that was the direction she needed to go. She shut the hatch on her pod, and pulled the straps of her pack together as she marched out. Snow covered terrain stretched before her, the landscape rougher than she had assumed.

She'd need all of the two hours she'd allowed herself to get to the castle. The entire mission now seemed more dangerous. A snow storm could blow in and blind her, and she didn't have enough protection for that, let alone the ability to find the pod if she had to. She hesitated, wondering if she should keep going.

Climbing up a steep snow bank, she caught a glimpse of lights on the horizon.

No, there was the city. It would take some time to get there, but she could do it.

She would do it.

CHAPTER TWENTY-TWO

Kelvaras stood at the back of the Ops room, closest to the door, one leg resting on the frame, his arms crossed as he surveyed the room. Tyron stood at the front, ready to update everyone on the plans for a reconnaissance of the Crown City. The room was alive with whispers of anticipation as people kept arriving. But there was one person missing. One vital person.

Tyron glanced over at Kelvaras.

"Where's Vyvica?" Tyron mouthed, his eyebrows bunched down low over his eyes. Kelvaras shrugged, his gaze searched the room, but he already knew she wasn't there. He hadn't *felt* her presence.

Tyron excused himself from the group that were having a discussion and approached him. Kelvaras watched him as he navigated the groups of people carrying on their own conversations.

"Have you not seen her?"

"Not since the incident last week. She's made herself scarce around me."

Tyron checked around the room, worry creasing his forehead. Kelvaras' heart did a double beat as a sinking feeling pulled in his gut.

"Can you go and check her quarters?" Tyron asked.

"I... I don't know where they are. And if she's there, I'm the last person she'll want to see."

"I don't care if you are. Her room is on the third level, Room 17. Here is the chip to enter. Knock first though, won't you."

"Will certainly do that, don't want my neck snapped." Kelvaras grinned at him, but the worry lines deepened on Tyron's face. He left without farewell and headed straight to her quarters.

He knocked on the door.

"Vyv- Commander, it's me, you have a meeting to attend." He called out.

Silence filled the room, his own breathing the only sound in the hallway, which sounded loud to him.

"Commander?" He called out again, pounding on her door.

Still nothing.

He used the card to access her room. The sparseness of it surprised him.

Obviously she isn't one to hoard and collect.

Her bed remained neatly folded. Her desk clear of all but an electronic notepad. He checked it, but she hadn't left a note there. He checked her ensuite, knocking loudly, but he couldn't hear the steam shower.

"Vyvica?" He called out. The sound echoed slightly around the spartan room. "Just where have you gone?" He wondered aloud. Turning on his heels, he went down to the training room.

Empty.

No sign of her logging in.

Alarm flared within him and his stomach churned uneasily. She'd been particularly moody since he'd tackled her in the Ops Room. He'd humiliated her, but she needed to know that she had to use her head first before allowing her emotions to move her into action. Sometimes holding back was the key.

She'd been adamant that he'd completed his job, and as far as he was aware, he had, but Tyron had kept him on hand. The D'Authian Guard would be in Ch'ar's hand soon enough, if they were planning a reconnaissance, then surely they were planning on an invasion. Mind you, from what he had gathered from Vyvica and Tyron, they had been planning on re-entering the City for the last five years. Ch'ar hadn't planned on invading Elador, and he wasn't going to tell Tyron that.

Feathers of fear tickled inside his stomach, and a cold crawling sensation started at the base of his scalp. He chided himself, but there was something about Vyvica. He wasn't going to betray her. But he wasn't sure how he could keep her away from Althu if she thought her father was there.

And who was her father?

"Where are you, Vyvica?" he asked the air around him.

He felt drawn to check the pod park. He wasn't sure why, but a strong desire made him move towards the area.

Vyvica's pristine pod was nowhere to be seen. He ran from mechanic bay to mechanic bay, and no sign of her pod. Worry brought a chill to his spine as he ran back inside the warehouse to the Ops Room.

The meeting was well underway and silence filled the room as he burst in.

"Her pod's gone," he interrupted, looking directly at Tyron.

"Who's gone?" Someone at the front of the room asked, but the look on Tyron's face told him all he needed to know. She'd gone to the Crown City on her own.

Tyron hurried towards him, pulling him out of the room as he went.

"Her pod is gone? Was there any message in her room?"

"No. Are we able to track her pod?"

"There's a positioning system on board."

"Will it be activated?"

"It's always activated," Tyron said as they hurried down the corridor to the Comms Room. He tapped the pad and the doors whooshed open. He pulled Kelvaras in behind him as he entered.

"Can you locate Commander Karala's vessel, please," he said, gripping a young officer on the shoulder, his knuckles white and shaking

"Yes, sir," the officer said. A screen with the current topographical map sat in front of him. The map moved as it searched for the locator beacon on Vyvica's pod. A repeated blip on the screen showed the location.

"The pod is an hour out from the Crown City and"—" the young man responded, he paused for a moment, studying the map. "The vessel is stationary."

"Damned woman!" Tyron spluttered angrily. Kelvaras looked from Tyron's pale face to the screen and back.

"I'll go," Kelvaras said. His vessel sat in the hidden warehouse park, but he knew he wouldn't get to her within an hour. It was a twelve hour journey, even at top speed. But he'd as much chance as she of getting into the castle. In fact, he would be able to get in without too much hassle at all and hopefully...he swallowed hard.

Could he get to her before she got in, without having to reveal himself to Ch'ar? Now that she'd put herself into the hands of Ch'ar—where he was supposed to deliver her—he didn't want her there. He wanted her safe, in *his* arms, where she *should* be, because no matter what she thought of him, he liked her and needed her.

He wanted to fight alongside her to get the Realm of Elador back into the King's control.

Not hand her over to Ch'ar.

He didn't need Ch'ar's money, he didn't want it.

At that moment he took sides for the first time in his life.

Tyron cut into his thoughts. "That's too big a risk for you alone."

"I'm a vigilante for hire, don't you think I'm capable of doing such a job?" His tone cooled as he spoke, heat rising in his cheeks and he gritted his teeth as he tried to keep his temper in check.

Tyron nodded. "Sorry. You go, we'll send support." He sighed, suddenly looking grey and tired. "The invasion is going to happen sooner than we thought."

"Hold off sending the troops in. If you don't hear from me within twenty-three hours, then send them in."

"Twenty-three hours?"

"It gives me a chance to do reconnaissance too, sir. If I can't get in, then we'll have to make a plan, but if you don't hear from me, there might be two of us that need rescuing."

"Are you sure?"

Kelvaras glared at Tyron. The older man patted him on the shoulder.

"She's my responsibility. I should go after her."

"You're the second-in-command. Can't have Ch'ar holding both of you. Stay here. And why would she be your responsibility? She's a woman in her own right."

"You don't understand her importance. One day, perhaps-"

"Her importance? Tell me now. It could be something I need to know," he said, his voice rising. Tyron paled under the younger man's glare. "Tell me now. I don't want to be walking into a very nasty situation."

Tyron pulled him out of the Comms Room, where they were gaining the attention of everyone. The door shut behind them with a slight hiss, and Tyron looked up and down the corridor.

"This is strictly confidential, you understand?"

"Yes!"

"Vyvica Karala is of importance, especially to Ch'ar."

"I already know that." Kelvaras' stomach clenched tightly. He raised his hands and gripped the older man on the shoulders, prepared to shake the answer out of him, but the comment triggered a memory. A recalled conversation he'd had with Ch'ar. Now that he thought about it, he was after someone in particular.

Tyron sighed, looking decidedly uncomfortable. "Vyvica is the king's daughter."

"What?" Kelvaras exploded. All of the conversations came into clarity. The closeness between Tyron and Vyvica became clearer.

He was her bodyguard.

"Shit." The full impact of her decision to run hit him.

Did Ch'ar know that she's the princess?"

"Tyron, I have something to tell you."

Tyron raised his eyebrows. Kelvaras let his hands drop to his side. He turned and paced away, sweeping his hand across his forehead.

"I... I'm working for Ch'ar." He held up his hands to stop Tyron from reacting, but decided to talk fast instead. "Ch'ar engaged my services to find your group, but I didn't realise why. Now I know. He wanted Vyvica, because she would know who the princess was. I don't think he knows who Vyvica really is. There may be a chance I can get her out before Ch'ar knows she's there."

"How can I trust you?" Tyron exploded. He paced back and forth in the hallway, his hand resting on his chest.

"Ch'ar will kill Vyvica, unless I can get to her first. I can't let that happen—I won't let that happen."

"Why would he kill her?"

"Because he wants information, and she is pigheaded enough not to supply it to him. I'm the only one that can rescue her from herself. You *have* to trust me, Tyron."

"I don't see why I should."

"You're going have to."

CHAPTER TWENTY-THREE

Her feet were heavy and each step grew painful. How long did it take to trek through snow? Vyvica looked down and saw that her soles were thick with compacted snow, even though they were covered in spikes. No wonder walking was a strain. Her hands were tucked underneath her armpits. Even with fur lined gloves, they were frozen. She had underestimated how long it would take, but she could see the city and focused on it. Vyvica wasn't sure what she planned to do once she got there, although warming up would be a good start.

The Crown City glowed in the growing darkness. There hadn't been a snow storm or blizzard, which was fortunate, or she would be dead.

Each footstep brought her closer to the warm interior of her former home. Every step brought her closer to her goal; to find her father.

It took another hour before she reached out and touched the wall, which she did with a cry of relief. She wanted to sink down against it, but she knew she couldn't stay there—she had to press on.

The large rock wall radiated coldness. An image of the entry points sprang to mind, and from the direction she faced, probably about half an hour from where she stood. Without wasting time she painstakingly edged her way towards the back of the Crown City, hoping that the entranceway she looked for had not been covered with a thick layer of snow and ice.

Feeling the mortar spaces between the large blocks, Vyvica counted how many there were. She didn't know exactly how many, but there was a mortar space slightly wider than the others. Her fingers trailing along picked up one that felt thicker. She went back to it and felt around the edge of the block. Kneeling down, she dug through the piled up snow, trying to find the ground. Some of the old snow had compacted, making the surface hard to smash. Even the tool on her belt couldn't break through the solid ice.

Tears of frustration threatened to flow from her eyes, but she knew her goggles would fog up, and she couldn't afford to take them off. She blinked rapidly to dissipate the tears.

Filled with trepidation, she realised she needed to find another entrance.

Vyvica pushed on, looking above her, because she recalled the next entrance way higher up, which would be easier for her to access. She found the vent, higher on the wall, and it was tiny. When she was little, she'd made it through. As an adult, that wouldn't happen.

She huffed out a breath and rubbed at her face, the extreme cold numbing her senses, her thoughts were scattering and meaningless and starting to blur.

Getting in was a priority.

Little by little, her extremities were starting to cool and move slower. She wouldn't last another hour outside. She hurried to the next entrance. Running in the thick snow was near impossible, but freezing to death wasn't an option.

The third vent was another ground one, but she couldn't open it, not even with the knife clipped to her belt. The ice had frozen the bolt and corroded it shut. Anxiety kept her going, but things weren't looking hopeful. Unwilling to collapse in the snow, Vyvica trudged to the next secret entranceway.

The block door, concealed within the wall, was almost invisible in the mortar and ice. The wider mortar space gave it away, slightly higher than she remembered, but accessible. Hope burned within her as she held her breath and willed her arms to have the strength to find the right hole, the access point. She put her gloved fingertips on the edge and pulled with all her might. She felt it give a little, enough to give her encouragement.

Her nostrils flared as anger and adrenaline flooded through her, and she used the heat in her head and heart to tug away at the block. The knife eased the opening out of its block enclosure, millimetre by millimetre. She wanted to laugh, but the job wasn't finished yet. She still had to get the door open and climb inside. With no exterior surveillance, she hoped to enter the castle in no time. Surely if there were someone watching she would've been apprehended by now.

Persistence kept her at it, and after a further half an hour, and constant repositioning of her fingers and the knife, she eased the door out enough for her to clamber through. Once in, however, there was no way for her to close the opening. With no handle or knobs or anything to grasp and pull towards her, she eased the door as closed as she could with the knife.

It was an escape hatch, not an entry point. She hoped that it wasn't too obvious, but a very cold draught pushed through the opening, finding gaps within her clothing.

She crawled through the dank, dark tunnel. Light didn't penetrate past her body. She took her torch out to illuminate the way. The harsh bright light made her blink as her eyes adjusted. Circular patterns glimmered in the torchlight as it shone down the long straight tunnel. Vyvica couldn't recall this tunnel as one that she played in as a child, but she remembered Tyron being behind her, and he was taller then than she was now, so she knew she would easily fit through. But where did it come out?

She banged her head sharply on a dead end in the tunnel and she eased her arm up to rub the sore spot. She'd been so focused on trying to remember where all the different tunnels came out, that she hadn't noticed the tunnel end and the hole above her head. She looked up and found a ladder. She unsnapped the snood from around her mouth and took a couple of breaths, and found the air cold but not below freezing, holding the torch clamped in her mouth, her hands free to climb.

CHAPTER TWENTY-FOUR

The top of the tunnel ended with a grate into a dark room. She stayed confined within the corridor, listening, but not hearing much over the pounding of her heart. She still couldn't remember where this tunnel originated.

The room above was silent, and the longer she waited, the colder her fingers got. Looking up, Vyvica couldn't see anything. She took a breath and shone her torch up onto the ceiling, showing her a dark red. Most of the interior of the City had the same coloured ceiling, making it familiar to her, but it didn't indicate where in the Palace she was.

With no movement outside the vent, she took another breath and galvanised her courage before easing the grate free. Vyvica pulled herself up as quietly as she could, replacing the large steel cover.

A cold draught pushed up through the lattice, chilling her face. Rubbing her gloved hands together and stamping her feet to bring the blood back, she looked around using the torch to light it up, the room remained unfamiliar. Large, hermetically sealed crates were stacked against one wall. A small memory of a store room stirred, but a lot of the basement had been storage. Her memory failure surprised her.

She'd lived and breathed in this City, been to its deepest depths and highest points, had clambered in and out of most of the escape tunnels, but the memory of which part of the castle she was in eluded her.

How could she have forgotten so much in five years? Glancing at her positioning unit, she determined that she was in the storage facility in the back quarter of the city. Last time she'd played through this area of the castle, this room had stored food.

Vyvica crept to the door and listened quietly, wondering what, if anything, was going on out in the corridor. Nothing stirred or moved, not that she could hear much through the blast door. She wished she'd brought surveillance equipment, but the bulky gear would have slowed her down.

Dusk had been falling as she found her way into the castle, so she presumed it would be pitch black outside now. Back at Apos, they would have had their meeting, had dinner, slept and would be starting to have their breakfast.

With a pang of guilt she wondered what Kelvaras and Tyron were doing right now.

Would they have noticed her missing yet?

They were twelve hours behind The Crown City of Althu. She smiled as she thought about how she had outsmarted both Kelvaras and Tyron.

Her smile faded.

Have I outsmarted them?

What had she planned to do once she got here?

Find my father.

What if he wasn't here? Their intelligence hadn't verified he was alive, let alone being held here. He could've been moved. She didn't want to consider the alternative – she shuddered – that he was dead.

Father can't be dead.

They hadn't found any sign of him anywhere else.

Maybe Kelvaras was right. She did act without thinking. Why did she do that? And now she was within the castle walls, without a plan. But she didn't fancy going back outside, especially in the dark. How did she manage to get herself into such fixes? She could hear Kelvaras tell her *'it's because you're pig-headed.'* She suppressed a nervous giggle. Yep, he was right.

She was inside now, and she had to figure out the quickest and quietest way to get to the heart of the castle. She listened once more at the door, knowing it was a fruitless effort, she had to assume it was safe...or as safe as it was going to be. She removed the glove from her left hand, and held it up against the scan pad. A green light outlined her hand and the latch clicked.

Too late, she realised that it would log in at the central computer. She cursed her own stupidity as the door slid open. Her breath stolen from her lungs, and her heart beating a tattoo within her chest, she checked the corridor before hurrying out, hoping to head in the southern direction, trying to distance herself from the room.

Almost immediately footsteps echoed around the halls, lots of them, clipping along the corridor behind her. Adrenaline flooding her muscles, she tried to identify a crack, a door, a number, anything that would lead her back to something familiar, a doorway, a picture, anything that would tell her where she was.

Shouts echoed from the corridor, disorienting her. Confused, she crept along, aware that they were probably separating out and trying to locate her now.

Damn, she wished she'd had a plan.

There wasn't even anywhere she could hide.

Five years didn't seem like long enough to forget, but she hadn't taken into account the damage done to the city back when the attack happened, or how the repairs might have changed the layout. She didn't want to get more lost, but there was no choice.

She kept moving.

Voices rose and fell, getting closer, fading away. She had no intention of giving herself up.

CHAPTER TWENTY-FIVE

Kelvaras hated flying at night, especially in a machine he was not used to. Tyron had insisted that he take one of the pods, rather than his own vessel. He didn't argue, because the pod would definitely be faster. He had thought about taking it to where Vyvica had left her vessel, and hoping she'd still be on board, but he knew she wouldn't be.

Pig-headed woman!

There was only one other option.

He pushed the button on his personal communicator.

"Kelvaras. It's about time you provided me with an update," Ch'ar said.

"Good news, I guess."

"You guess?"

"Vyvica Karala is within range of the City."

"Althu?"

"Yes. Her vessel's parked up near the city, we suspect she is making her way towards it, could already be in it."

"We?"

"The D'Authian Guard and I."

"Right. And where're you now?"

"On my way."

"Good. I'll see you soon then."

"Yes." He clicked off the communicator then sighed heavily.

He suspected that Ch'ar already knew Vyvica was close by, or he already had her.

Something in his tone.

He hadn't sounded surprised enough.

Just what was he playing at?

Damn her.

Once more she was proving to him exactly what he thought all along, she acted first, planned later.

Such a dangerous game to play.

Why did he care?

But his heart had already chosen sides and he had to follow its lead.

CHAPTER TWENTY-SIX

The rhythmic clomp of running boots drew closer and Vyvica slipped into an open doorway. She squatted down, listening as the footsteps approached and retreated. She breathed out, closed her eyes and inhaled, trying to steady the buzzing in her ears. She continued to listen, but the corridor went quiet.

Nothing-moving-quiet.

Standing up, she brushed dust from her jacket and stepped out of the doorway, straight into a stationary object. A hand grabbed her arm in a painful grip. She wasn't certain whether it was steadying her or capturing her, but it stopped her from stumbling backwards.

"Commander Karala, I presume." She looked up. Her gaze kept climbing the solid chest and finally into the dark intimidating cowl of his cloak. His face remained hidden in the shadows of the corridor, only the whites of his eyes penetrated the gloom. But she knew who he was.

"Yes, I am," she said, trying to inject some coldness into her voice. There wasn't any point in denying who she was. The one person she'd hoped to avoid and she'd managed to end up in his clutches.

"I've been waiting for you."

Vyvica tried to twist out of his hold, but it tightened around her arm, threatening to cut off the circulation. "Have you." It wasn't a question.

"Yes, Commander Karala. I understand that you've come alone." How did he know? The information stunned Vyvica. His iron grip on her wrist intensified as he turned and walked her down the corridor.

"I have someone who's been waiting a long time to see you. But I think you need to freshen up first." He pulled her through a labyrinth of corridors, twisting and turning her around so much she had no idea where she was.

The interior of the Castle had changed since she'd left.

"Where are you taking me?"

"Somewhere comfortable."

"But I was comfortable back there." Again she tried to pull out of his grip. He turned and growled at her, a menacing cold sound.

"You aren't leaving. It's taken me five years to get you here, now I have you, I don't intend to let you go until you give me what I need."

"What do you need?"

"Oh you know, the usual stuff. Where you're based, who's in your employ—no wait, I already know all of that."

"Who? Who told you?"

"Several of your people, actually. I have had my own people inside your networks the entire time. They were right under your nose and you didn't even know."

"We knew about Siara."

"Siara is only one person. And you only found out about her because I wanted you to."

"One? How many more are there?"

"Now, I don't think you're in a position to ask such questions."

Vyvica stopped in her tracks, jerking Ch'ar to a halt. "I think I'm entitled to know who the traitors are."

"That's a fair comment. But there's no point in telling you now. I need to know where the princess is. Only you know where she is."

Vyvica's face went cold and dread crawled up her spine, raising the hairs on the back of her neck.

"Don't you know where she is?"

A steely look crept into his stare. "No. None of my informants could find her. Apparently there are only two people who know; the commander of the D'Authian Guards, and her bodyguard, Tyron." His tone lowered with each syllable until it was an urgent whispered threat.

Vyvica's mouth went dry as she realised the full implications. With all the resources within the city, Ch'ar hadn't been able to determine who the princess was. She didn't want to blurt it out to him, she'd been sworn to secrecy, but her heart skipped a beat.

It was worse than she first thought.

Her chest and face burned with indignation and humiliation. She pulled against him, but his grip tightened.

"I *am* stronger than you, Vyvica."

"That is *Commander Karala* to you," she said through gritted teeth as she pulled her weight behind her and kicked out with her left leg. Ch'ar anticipated her move and caught her foot, lifting it above her head. Balancing precariously while hopping on her other foot, Vyvica maintained her balance.

"Now what're you going to do?" Ch'ar smirked at her. Her cheeks heated as she gritted her teeth. She could hear Kelvaras' own words ringing in her ears.

"No matter what you do, I'm one step ahead of you. I know that you're an expert in hand to hand combat, but you fail to realise that I'm faster and stronger than you, and you're quick to react. If you value your life, *Commander Karala*, you will do as you're told. If you do, the pain will be less, and your life will end more quickly. Do you understand me?" Ch'ar's voice chilled her.

Vyvica swallowed the cold fear that crawled around her scalp, making her hair prickle. She took a deep breath, trying to remain calm, but the pulse in her wrist where he held her would no doubt give away her quickened heartbeat. She nodded, not trusting her voice. He let go of her foot, and she slowly lowered it to the ground, trying to show him the power she had over her muscles. He nodded as he considered the movement, but never took his gaze from her eyes.

She was physically and mentally trapped.

Tightening his grip on her wrist, he waited a moment before marching down the corridor, quickly catching up with a group of guards who had been looking for her. Vyvica couldn't help but smirk at the look of surprise on their faces.

"You lot are incompetent. She ducked into a room that you walked right past without even checking." He didn't yell; his voice was icy and quiet.

"Sorry, Lord Ch'ar," the leader of the group said. His face was unmasked, unlike the rest of the armed guards. The man's uniform was the same as the others, except there were more epaulets on his shoulder.

"You will be," Ch'ar addressed the head of the group.

"Yes, Lord Ch'ar," he replied, turning his cold stare onto Vyvica. She shuddered from the hatred radiating from them.

"Take her to the interrogation room. And watch her feet, they're very quick. I'll be there presently." He dropped her wrist and she instinctively reached for it with her other hand, rubbing the coldness from it.

Two men stepped forward and grabbed an arm each, their grip painful on the tender flesh of the underarms. She pulled against them, but they wrestled her and clamped her into a double team hold, her shoulders pinned back. The circulation in her hands tightened and her hands started to tingle.

It was fruitless to resist. She would only tire more quickly. Best to conserve her energy, because she didn't know what he intended to do, or what form the interrogation would take.

The head of the group stepped in front of her. He leaned in close, his lip curling up in a snarl. He spat in her face, making her blink a couple of times.

"You're a trouble-making little bitch aren't you." A gloved hand came up and caressed her face before it withdrew. A flash of black and her cheek erupted in white-hot pain. Looking back at him, she stretched her jaw to try and relieve the pain.

"That's for getting us in trouble. And this"—" He punched her in the stomach; all of the wind went out of her lungs and her legs collapsed under her. "Is also for getting us into trouble. There is plenty more of that to come," he said, and she could hear the smile in his voice. The two guards dragged her as she tried to move her legs, but breath wasn't coming into her lungs, no matter how much she tried to draw it in.

Vyvica didn't recall passing out, but a bucket of ice-cold water certainly woke her. She shrieked in protest, realising she wore her tank top and leggings, which were now saturated and fast getting cold.

Her arms were tied above her head and she leaned forward at a funny angle. The muscles in her shoulders protested at holding her own weight. She tried to move her feet forward to ease the ache, but they wouldn't budge. She shook the water from her hair, which lay in wet tendrils around her shoulders.

Vyvica took a moment to observe her surroundings; a dark room, lit behind her by a fire, she presumed because of the flickering light, which wasn't warming her. Her teeth chattered.

"Hello Vyvica, pleased you could join us." Ch'ar moved into her field of vision. Her gaze strained to follow him as he moved in front of her. Her body shivered violently as the chill settled into her bones.

Ch'ar walked around her, making her feel like a specimen being inspected. He reached out and rubbed her arm, feeling the muscles, running his hand down her side and along her thigh to her knee. She tried to flinch from his touch, but movement was restricted. Ch'ar laughed, a chilling sound.

"Have you not got anything to say?" he asked from behind her. She kept her mouth closed.

A crack sounded and pain exploded across her back. She screamed.

Her skin burned and increased with each passing second.

"Every time you don't answer, you will get that. Do you understand me?"

Vyvica tried to nod her head, but couldn't. Her breath hadn't come back into her lungs.

A new pain surged through her scalp as Ch'ar grabbed a handful of her hair and wrenched her head backwards. The strain on her muscles made her body shake. Her windpipe closing with her head pulled back so far.

A strangled cry came out of her throat.

Ch'ar's breath huffed on her right ear and cheek, but she couldn't see him.

"Do you understand, Commander Karala?"

"Yes," she whispered hoarsely.

Crack!

Another intense flash of pain slashed across her rump.

"I didn't hear you."

"Yes!" She cried out, gasping for each lungful of air. He let go and her head fell forward, her breath rasping as she dragged in as much air as she could.

"That's better. Now, since you're the head of the D'Authian Guard, you're privy to information that I'm after. Tell me, Commander, where is the princess?"

"I don't know."

Crack!

"I don't know!"

Crack!

She sobbed.

With each searing strike from the whip, she screamed, her back ablaze.

Tears streamed down her face as she kept whispering, "I don't know. I don't know. I don't know," like a mantra. She focused on each word, trying to forget the agony that exploded across her back, blood dripping down her shredded shirt. She let her head hang forward, it hurt too much to keep it up.

"Sir?" She heard a voice behind her, but couldn't make out the urgent whispering that ensued. Shreds of her shirt were moved away from her shoulder blades, and then Ch'ar took a sharp intake of breath and cursed.

"Well, either you don't know who you really are, or you're a fool," Ch'ar announced behind her.

She closed her eyes, cringing, expecting to feel the lash of the whip once more, but it never came. Ch'ar strode around in front of her; all she could see were his black trousers and boots. He grabbed her hair and pulled her head upright to look at him, she could barely see through her tear swollen eyes.

"You could've saved your beautiful skin and told me who you were in the first place."

"I'd rather die." She lobbed a ball of spit at him. He blinked, and laughed, wiping his face.

"That can be arranged. But for now, your skin is safe." He muttered to the men behind her and he left with a swish of his long jacket.

Gentle hands lifted her arms up and the cuffs were removed. They eased her upright, but her body remained off balance. She clung to the arm of the man who supported her and gave her the courtesy of not touching her shredded back. They unchained her ankles and the two guards escorted her from the dungeon-like room, but out in the corridor she realised that she hadn't been in the basement at all.

Across the hall, the door to a medic unit stood open and the two guards eased her into the light. She blinked repeatedly, her eyes trying to adjust to the brightness. She sobbed as they sat her on the bed.

"It's okay, your highness." One of the visored men told her. The other one hit him on the shoulder.

"What? He told us to take care of her," he replied to the one that had hit him.

Vyvica held up her hand, as high as the pinching burn in her back would allow, indicating for them to shut up.

"Please, just go." She couldn't ignore the burning sensation of her back and between that and the arguing, she couldn't be bothered.

"You may leave us. Wait outside the door, I will send for you when I'm finished." The medic stated as he entered the room. He waited as the men hesitated, before they left the room.

Vyvica didn't recognise the medic as he clucked his tongue several times; she could hear his feet shuffling around behind her, 'tsking' a few times.

Vyvica sat statue-still, her hands in her lap; studying the back of her hands. She didn't feel sorry for herself; the pain absorbed all of the emotions. Anger and pity were non-existent.

By being the princess, she'd gained some time.

But how much?

"I'm just going to cut away your shirt." The medic's soft voice interrupted her thoughts. She held her arms across her chest to maintain her dignity. She watched as strips of her shirt fell to her side. Bile rose as she noted the amount of blood on the cloth.

"How bad is it?" She hissed through teeth clenched to hold back the pain.

"Bad enough, I'm afraid." The cutting of fabric had stopped as the medic studied her. Warm, gentle hands moved over her back with the occasional pull and sting as he peeled strips of material caught in the congealing blood. He dropped them onto a bowl beside her.

"Does it hurt much?"

She choked on a laugh. "Yeah, it hurts like a bitch." Warmth flooded over her back, and a bright light threw her shadow onto the wall and floor in front of her.

"I have the laser on it. It will help to cauterise the blood vessels and that should stem the flow of blood."

"It's still bleeding?" she asked, but she already knew.

"Yes, but that will stop. The laser will dry it and the scabs will fall off. You'll be left with scar tissue, and it will be tender for a few days, but you'll survive. A few scars though, I'm afraid."

"Just adds to my character," Vyvica replied dryly. She heard the medic chuckle, to her surprise.

"Must remember that one," he said. He came and stood in front of her. His dark grey eyes glanced over her face and down her body as he checked her over. The creased skin around his eyes told her he was experienced.

He sighed. "You're a very lucky young lady. It shouldn't affect your muscles, but there's some superficial damage. It would pay to take a few days before you start training again."

"I somehow don't believe they'll let me do any training." She smiled, but knew it didn't reach her eyes. The medic gently gripped her shoulder.

"You're probably right. Well, just make sure you don't do anything strenuous for a few days."

Vyvica clutched at her shredded top, keeping it in place over her breasts and held out a hand, the medic gripped gently and shook it.

"Thank you. For your kindness."

"Not everyone supports Lord Ch'ar," he whispered to her. He went behind her and checked on the progress. The light switched off.

"You'll feel some tingles and twitches as the nerve endings reconnect, and you may feel some stretching in the skin as it heals. I'll visit you tomorrow and check on progress."

"Thank you." The medic left the room and the two guards returned. They went to take an arm each.

"I don't have enough arms to keep this up." She looked at the tattered remains of her top. "And I want to keep my dignity, so perhaps one walks in front, one walks behind and you can lead me to wherever you want to go." They seemed reluctant.

"Look, I'm not in any fit state to try and escape now, am I?" Because they were both visored, she hoped that she looked at the one that had been kind to her earlier. One nodded to the other, and she slid to the edge. Unaware that she had been barefoot, the cold seeped up through her feet as she eased off the bed.

"Do you think I might get some warm clothes?" she asked tentatively. She didn't expect an answer, but she hoped that they would listen or bring her some.

CHAPTER TWENTY-SEVEN

They led her to a large room, holding only a bed and a chair. A change of clothes lay on the bed, and someone stood looking out a small slit of a window. Clutching the scraps of cloth to her chest, she stepped cautiously through the door. Something familiar drew her to study the tall man; the stoop of his shoulders was new, the curl of the now grey hair at his collar, and his clothes weren't as tidy and presentable as she'd expect them to be.

"Dad?" she asked cautiously and the figure at the window turned.

"My precious child, is that really you?" His voice a barely audible whisper.

As she drew closer, she saw his pale face lined with years of worry, but it was definitely her father.

She couldn't tell for certain, it could have been her eyes, but she thought she saw...a flicker? Perhaps it was the artificial light in the room.

Her father opened his arms and stepped towards her, pulling her into his arms.

"Careful, Dad," she said through gritted teeth as his hands touched the tender skin on her back. He looked at her, concern etched on his face, but she leaned back into him, tears stinging her eyes. She didn't want to talk about it. Her father eased his hands onto her back and she found warmth and comfort in his hug.

Something she had not felt in a long time and she let out a sob.

"Father?" She couldn't quite comprehend it. He held her for a long time. She inhaled, trying to remember his scent, but it seemed... non-existent. No peppery smell of his soap, or the raw odour of sweat. Nothing. Even his clothes did not smell like they had been laundered. Confusion caused her to pull away.

"Let me look at you." He held her at arms-length and looked her up and down. He reached out a hand and brushed a stray strand of hair back from her face.

"Why did you come back?" he asked.

"I had to come and get you."

"Where is the rest of the team?"

"They're coming."

"How soon?" His eyes narrowed a little, not one of his usual facial quirks, but then it had been five years. A lot could happen in that time.

"As soon as they can. I'm part of the scouting party." She lied, she didn't know why, but she didn't want anyone to know she'd come on her own.

"How many of you are there?"

"Why twenty questions, Dad? Aren't you happy to see me?"

"I am, my love, I am. Just making sure that backup is coming." He pulled her into his arms and hugged her tightly.

Vyvica nodded, but something didn't seem right, her father wasn't normally so demonstrative. She looked down at her top.

"Do you mind...if I change?"

"No, go right ahead." But he didn't turn around to give her privacy.

"Turn around please, Dad." Her cheeks flamed.

"Oh, sorry love." He turned, and looked out the window again. She hastily threw the shredded top aside and pulled on the dress that had been provided. She winced as it came in contact with the cut skin on her back, but the sensation passed.

The dress felt awkward and bulky around her legs, but she kept her leggings on. She pulled on the fastenings on the front, tightening the bodice, preferring not to have the fabric moving across her tattered back. She tugged at the low cut of the top, hoping to pull it up, but to no avail.

"All right," she said, reluctantly smoothing the fabric down.

"My, aren't you just a pretty thing." Her father admired her. She frowned as she watched him. Again she thought she saw a flicker within his image, her gaze moved to the lighting, a buzzing hum filtered through the silent room. As she watched, a flicker occurred. Definitely the lights.

"Come my dear, sit and tell me what you've been up to?" He took her hand and led her to the bed. She sat down beside him, allowing him to hold her hand, stroking it.

"What do you want to know?"

"Well, where've you been for the last five years?"

"The D'Authian Guard built up a resistance against Ch'ar. We nearly succeeded in bringing him down. I'm the leader of the D'Authian Guard now."

"You have been busy, haven't you?"

"Where've you been? You look old, but not too worse for wear."

He smiled kindly at her, even though she'd insulted him. He wouldn't have stood for similar comments prior to the invasion. "They've kept me contained within my apartments. When Ch'ar told me that they'd found you, I had to come and see you for myself. Did you tell him you're my daughter?"

"No, he found the mark. He had me whipped to give him the information on where the princess was. I stayed quiet, but someone recognised the birthmark." She looked down at their joined hands, her fingers toying with the veins on the back of his hand.

"My dear child. I'm sorry you had to endure that."

"Did they whip you, too?" She asked, curious to know what he'd experienced while in the hands of Ch'ar.

Her father shrugged. "No. But I was put in the dungeon for a while."

"What does Ch'ar want?"

"He wants me to sign an agreement for him to mine resources from our planet. He also wants more voting rights at the Intergalactic Senate."

"Why hasn't he mined it and taken it anyway?" Her eyebrows drew down over her eyes, curious to know why he hadn't just stripped what he needed and left.

"Because it is worthless to him if he sells it; it has to be certified as genuine and legally acquired."

"We can't let him, this is our planet, not his."

"Now that you're here, he has a bargaining chip. I won't be able to hold out if he threatens you."

"Father, you have to. You can't let him do this. You can't sign that agreement."

"But I don't want to see you hurt, Vivvy." She smiled at her father's use of the pet name, one that she didn't allow others to use.

"Father, you can't just give away our resources. They're ours, not his. You can stop him by not signing, Dad. I can hold out, don't worry about me." She knew her words sounded stronger than she felt. Her heartbeat increased knowing that their deaths were imminent.

Her father patted her hand kindly and shrugged. Her anger wasn't going to get her anywhere.

Loud voices echoed outside the door, interrupting the discussion. She looked at her father, then at the door, which she reached in three steps. She pressed her ear to the door and listened.

A commotion and yelling in the corridor, she couldn't make out the words, but she froze when she heard a familiar voice.

CHAPTER TWENTY-EIGHT

Kelvaras marched through the corridors, calling out as he went. A large contingent of guards trailed behind him, trying to pass and stop him, but he wouldn't be stopped.

"Ch'ar!" he bellowed. Finally, two guards halted him in the corridor next to the medical unit.

"Where is he?"

"He's coming, sir."

"So is the Festival of Snow." Kelvaras' anger rose. Sweat beaded on his forehead as he stripped off his jacket. He paced in the confined space that the guards allowed him.

"Ahhh, Kelvaras, lovely to see you again," Ch'ar said, approaching Kelvaras with his hand extended.

Kelvaras ignored it. "Where is she?" Anger punctuated his words.

"She?" Ch'ar shook his head and Kelvaras wanted to reach out and snap it off his neck.

"Vyvica, you know perfectly well who."

"Oh, her. She's my guest, for now."

"Guest! She didn't willingly come in here."

"Yes, she did. She entered the City of her own free will. However, you're right, but she's comfortable. For now."

"Where is she? I want to see her."

"Why would you want to see her?" Ch'ar smirked as he spoke, and Kelvaras clenched his fists, resisting the urge to punch him.

"I want to make sure she's all right."

"You can rest assured, she's perfectly fine."

"What are your plans for her?"

"She's my bargaining chip. She'll sign the treaty one way or another. Hopefully with her father's persuasion."

"But her father is-"

Ch'ar interrupted him. "Visiting with her now."

Kelvaras shook his head. "How..."

"Technology is a marvellous thing."

"What do you hope to accomplish?" Kelvaras put his hands on his hips and narrowed his eyes as anger resonated in his voice.

"To have the treaty signed. If she won't sign it, then I'll marry her...or kill her."

"She won't marry you." Kelvaras' voice rose.

"You seem very positive of that."

"I know she won't marry you. She'll marry me, though."

"Is that right, son."

"Don't call me that." Kelvaras hissed through his gritted teeth.

"Are you denying your birthright now too?"

"I'm not denying anything. But you haven't been a father to me before, why start now."

CHAPTER TWENTY-NINE

The word 'son' echoed through Vyvica's mind.

Kelvaras is Ch'ar's son?

Then that meant he was a traitor.

Vyvica's heart stopped in her chest. Her breath caught as a crushing blow hit her stomach. Her body trembled with the cold hard reality.

He'd been given information that would lead him to every one of her networks. She'd given him the information herself.

She fell to her knees.

Ch'ar's son?

Her heart ached.

A sob wracked her body.

Surely not.

Bile rose to the back of her throat.

She glanced over at her father, who remained sitting on the bed, passively watching her. Why hadn't he come over to her when she was clearly distressed?

The door opened and Kelvaras marched in, his eyes searching.

For her.

Vyvica rose shakily to her feet and glared at him.

Ch'ar slipped in behind him, smirking.

Vyvica wanted nothing more than to wipe that smile off his face.

Kelvaras' face lit up as he approached, but she slapped him across the face. Her fingers stung from the contact and she rubbed her hands together.

He pressed his palm to his cheek.

"What was that for?" His voice shook as he spoke.

"Deceiving me." She spat at him.

His face paled.

He looked from her to the door.

Vyvica closed her eyes.

"You heard?" His smooth voice a whisper.

She nodded. "Every word, you lying bastard." She opened her eyes, gazing at him, trying to ignore the pain in her chest. "You've lied to me and everyone else. Even yourself. You didn't tell us that you're the son of the man who invaded our planet." Vyvica flew at him, her hands clawing and scratching his face.

Ch'ar's laugh stopped her attack.

Kelvaras used the interruption to grab her hands and forced them behind her back, restraining her, pulling her into him. Her face against his chest, his scent filling her nostrils.

His comforting scent.

She struggled against him, another sob filling her.

Kelvaras smoothed her hair off her face as she puffed.

"She won't marry you, she'll marry me, instead." Kelvaras turned to Ch'ar.

"I'll see you both in hell first," she replied through clenched teeth. Ch'ar covered the distance from the doorway to her side with surprising speed.

"That can be arranged," Ch'ar hissed in her face.

"Do you mind? I'd like to talk to Vyvica. In private." Kelvaras moved to put himself between Vyvica and Ch'ar. Vyvica was thankful for the small movement.

Ch'ar, a nasty smile on his face, bowed low to them. "Good luck, Kelvaras. You'll need it." He backed out of the room, laughing.

The door shut with a solid clunk and Kelvaras looked at Vyvica. She could feel her heart racing in her chest, which rested against Kelvaras, sure he could feel it. He bent his head and kissed her.

His lips soft on hers, tender, but she didn't want to give in.

She bit and held his lip as he yelped at her.

"Vyvica, please."

She bit down harder before letting go. Kelvaras released her, and she stepped away as he reached up, checking his lip for blood.

"How dare you," she said,

"I'm here to make sure you're all right."

"I'd be a lot better if you weren't here." She paced the room.

"Seriously Vyvica, Ch'ar will kill you."

"I know he will, and I'll happily go to my death."

"Not if I can help it. Please Vyvica, you have to believe me."

"Why should I? What about Tyron? You've betrayed him, too." It wasn't a question.

"Tyron knows." He ducked his head down.

"Tyron?" Curses exploded from her mouth, at the same time as Kelvaras reached towards her, trying to talk over her tirade.

"Listen to me, I've only just told him. He was coming to get you, and I told him I would come. It was better for him to be the commander of the D'Authian Guards."

Vyvica turned her back to Kelvaras, tears rolling down her cheeks. She had been trying to trust him, it went against her gut instinct, to try and believe him.

"How can I tell if you're telling me the truth?" She cried, her tears flowing freely down her face.

"Vyvica, you have to trust me."

She shook her head. "I can't."

Movement told her that Kelvaras stood behind her. A hand touched her shoulder, gently. He turned her around.

"Vyvica, please." He bent his head towards hers, and he kissed her on the lips. A gentle kiss.

Part of her wanted to melt into his arms. Another part wanted to strangle the life out of the man. Her heart lay in shattered pieces within her chest. Why did her body still respond to him? He looked down into her eyes. She stepped back, her hands fluttered up to her mouth.

"Your guest is still sitting behind you."

Shocked, she turned around, and flushed, realising her father still sat on the bed. She'd forgotten about him.

"I'm..."

Her father's face remained blank, like he hadn't noticed the display of emotion.

"That's my father," she said, moving towards him.

"He isn't your father," Kelvaras said quietly, his hand reaching out to touch her shoulder. She shrugged it off and glared at him.

"He is my father."

"He's an illusion. Vyvica, your father is..."

"This is my father!" She was adamant. A smile creased the wrinkles around his eyes as Vyvica took his hand, softly caressing the paper-thin skin.

"No, he isn't."

"How dare you insult my lineage?"

"I'm not, Vyvica. You're the true princess, but that man there, he's an illusion. Your father is"—" He swallowed and paled. "Dead."

Vyvica shook her head, trying to deny it. Her eyes blurred with unshed tears. Something he said rang true, but she wanted to deny it.

"How can he be dead? I'm holding his hand," she sobbed.

Kelvaras walked up beside her, placing his hand in the small of her back. She tried to move away, but he pushed her. She tripped over the skirts of her dress and held up her hands to stop herself from falling onto her father. Instead, her hands went straight through him, he flickered then solidified once she moved out of the way. He continued to flicker as she watched, horrified.

Vyvica looked from her father, to Kelvaras.

"What's going on?" Pain and confusion exploded over her body, making her cold.

Feeling cornered, she backed up until she hit the wall and slid down, her arms curling around her knees, her head falling forward, allowing the tears to flow, dampening her skirts. She felt movement and heard the cracking of knees as Kelvaras squatted down in front of her. She felt him place a hand on her head, his fingers curling to push the hair back off her face.

"I'm on your side."

A bitter laugh escaped her. She shook her head.

"Look, Tyron's coming, and he's bringing the entire army. They'll infiltrate and bring weapons. Trust me on this," he whispered, resting his forehead on hers. Something in his tone made her look up. His eyes shone.

"How can I trust you?"

"If you don't, then Ch'ar will kill you. Your only option is to trust me."

She felt numb, her emotions deserted her. Her body a foreign object she couldn't control. Information overloaded her brain and she could no longer think clearly.

"Can you please leave me now?"

"I'd rather stay."

"I need some space. And take 'father' with you." She pointed to the flickering apparition on the bed.

CHAPTER THIRTY

The medic was the only person she saw. Since she'd been whipped, he'd systematically checked her dressings and by the second day, her back had healed enough for her to move, with a little tightness in the muscles.

By the fourth day, she had full range of movement, and she began exercising, phantom fighting, to keep her wits about her. She barely remembered each day passing, her mind occupied instead with her body and healing.

It had been five days since her confrontation with Ch'ar and Kelvaras. Kelvaras hadn't been back to see her, and the longer he stayed away, the more her nerves stretched.

Boredom would do her head in if she didn't get an opportunity to train. She cleared the room, leaving enough space to swing her leg around without it hitting something. Taking care of her back, and to make her training harder, she decided to do¬¬¬¬ everything in slow motion. The precise movements made her strain in a whole new way. The tension in her muscles lessened and she felt more relaxed, even if she lived under a death threat for refusing to marry Ch'ar or Kelvaras. To complicate things further were the full skirts she wore, the fabric heavy, providing good resistance.

The door swung open and Ch'ar entered, as he did the same time every day. She stopped and rose to her full height, ready to face anything.

"And how're you feeling today?"

"You don't want to know. Just get to the point."

"I wish my son was so easy to communicate with."

Vyvica crossed her arms and remained silent, waiting for Ch'ar to speak. He always made some comment about Kelvaras.

"All right, then. Sign the treaty."

"No."

"My patience is running short, Vyvica."

"Commander Karala to you, and I don't care how short your patience is. I won't sign the treaty. You'll not get the resources you want from this planet."

"You're well versed in the matter."

"You told me yourself."

He grabbed her face, drawing his own down to hers. His voice went cold. "If you don't sign it, I *will* put you to death."

"If you kill me, you'll not get your treaty signed. You won't be recognised as the ruler of this planet and our resources will remain worthless."

He grunted and shook her face, his grip painful on her cheekbones. "You're your father's daughter, aren't you?"

"He taught me well," she said, trying to smirk as his grip tightened. She wouldn't give him the satisfaction of letting him see her in pain.

"He taught you nothing. You know nothing of the political world outside of this planet." Spittle fell on her face.

"I'm well versed in most political matters. I know that you want the two senate votes that our planet is entitled to, this would increase your own voting rights, and it would also allow you to legalise the ownership of the resources from this planet, but I won't be a part of that, so I suggest you put me to death."

"You accept death so easily. Perhaps you don't believe I'll follow through with it."

A flutter of fear played in her stomach. He shook her face and let go, laughing at her. She wiped his spit from her face, he'd seen her fear and she chastised herself.

The steel coldness in his eyes made her wonder if perhaps she'd misjudged him. A smile spread across his face, and the hair and skin on her neck prickled. If she, as the sole surviving monarch, didn't have an heir, then the Intergalactic Senate would decide who would be the King or Queen. Ch'ar wouldn't be able to influence the Senate to make himself the King, surely. She swallowed the cold lump at the back of her throat and her hands fidgeted with her skirt folds.

"Well, *Commander Karala*, I suggest you prepare for your death, which will take place in two days' time."

"You don't scare me." She put as much bravado in her voice as she could.

"I'm not trying to."

Before Vyvica could respond, he bowed and left the room. She took a deep breath, closed her eyes and blew it out, trying to return her pulse to normal. As much as she could be staunch, she didn't want to die young.

The shutting of the door sounded like a death knell.

"Tyron, where are you?" she whispered to the empty room.

CHAPTER THIRTY-ONE

Kelvaras watched as Ch'ar stormed into the throne room, marching to the fire to warm his hands, cursing quietly.

"That woman will be the end of me! She's a hindrance. There's no other option. She has to die."

The words made Kelvaras' chest contract. He took a deep breath, trying to relieve the dread. "Let me talk to her."

Ch'ar paced back and forth across the throne room. "You think you can change her mind?"

"Probably not."

"Then there's nothing left but to execute her."

"You're not thinking this through. If you kill her, the Senate won't necessarily accept your claim to the Monarchy. We'll have to go ahead with your original plan, except I'll marry her."

"We? When did this become a 'we' business?"

"If you don't want my help"—""

"That isn't what I meant." Ch'ar heaved a sigh, looking around the room. "What will I gain if you marry her—other than an incredibly annoying daughter-in-law?"

"Always thinking about what you'll get out of any situation," Kelvaras grumbled.

"Don't change the topic."

"You'll get a *daughter-in-law* who's legally entitled to the throne," Kelvaras said, as he remained seated at the table.

Ch'ar continued to pace.

"And what will you gain out of it?"

"I'll be the husband of the Queen of Eldora. You might not have the authority to take over the planet, but you'll have a better position of power." Kelvaras watched as his father continued to pace. He didn't want to be on his side of the negotiations, but it was all he could think of to save the life of the woman he was falling in love with.

Falling in love with? When did that happen?

He stood up and approached the restless man, gripping his shoulders. "Ch'ar! I'll be married to the Queen of Eldora." Ch'ar stopped and looked him deep in the eye. "As the consort of the queen, I'll be able to get her to sign documentation..."

Slowly, Ch'ar's eyes lit up. Kelvaras sighed as he let go of the older man and returned to his seat.

Ch'ar started rambling on with his thoughts and ideas. As much as he wanted to share Ch'ar's enthusiasm, Kelvaras' thoughts were more to do with saving Vyvica. Hopefully she would trust him enough to agree to the marriage, although somehow he didn't think she would.

What could he do to convince her?

CHAPTER THIRTY-TWO

Kelvaras stood outside the door to her room and knocked. He didn't expect a response, so his heart leapt when he heard her call out.

He steeled himself as he opened the door, prepared for her to fly at him as he entered, but she didn't.

Instead she stood in the middle of her room, practicing her kicks in extreme slow motion. The precision and ease with which she moved mesmerised him. He closed the door and watched her fluid motions, contained and tight. The deliberateness of the extensions were graceful and he couldn't take his eyes of her sinewy limbs. A flush of warmth filled him and he smiled.

She looked up and a pretty, rosy glow filled her cheeks. But she didn't stop.

"When's my execution date?"

"It's not happening."

"Oh? Ch'ar seems keen to have me dead."

"It wouldn't suit his needs."

"Right. So what's the plan now?"

"We're getting married."

Vyvica burst out laughing, her leg falling to the ground, as she belly-laughed hard.

"You might think it's funny now, but if we don't marry, you will die."

"Given my options, death would be best." She placed her hands on her hips, her face going from pink to red.

"Come on Vyvica, you can't deny the attraction between us, the heat that runs through your body every time you're close to me. I've seen your blushes, the way you lick your lips."

Vyvica gasped. "That's an awfully big presumption. The only heat that runs through my body—"

He crossed the room and scooped her up in his arms. Before she could struggle or strain, he kissed her. The intensity seared through his body, transferring to hers. The kiss deepened, and she opened her mouth for him. Vyvica didn't struggle or push him away; instead she melded into his body. He pulled her tighter against him. The desire to drown in her strong.

The kiss ended naturally, and he looked down into her eyes. Warmth emanated from her gaze, boring into his. He wanted to get lost in those golden irises' which promised so much.

He wrapped his arms around her, pulling her tight to his chest, her mouth seeking out his again. Mouths meeting, his body tingled with a need that pooled in his groin. His lips fused to hers, he scrambled to lift the skirts to her hips, wanting desperately to feel her rubbing against his hardness. She wiggled in his arms, a sigh escaping as her pelvis pushed against him.

He had to have her.

He lifted her effortlessly and carried her to the bed, placing her down gently before kneeling over her, admiring her body.

Her liquid eyes were glazed with wanton lust and he knew he could be consumed by her brown gaze.

Vyvica laid her head back against the bedding, sighing as he rained kisses down her neck, his fingers fumbling with the ties confining her breasts. He untangled the leather laces, leaned down on an elbow, slowly peeling the fabric down to reveal two perfect breasts, the nipples tightening as they were exposed to the air.

He breathed in sharply.

She ground against him, and moaned as his tongue flicked over first one nipple, then the other, watching them draw into buds as goose-flesh erupted over her mocha coloured skin. Her hands crept into his hair, holding his head down to her breasts as he kissed and explored each one.

Vyvica starting tugging at his top, trying to pull it up over his head. She sat up, her hands fluttering over his chest before she pressed her mouth to his skin, her tongue trailing a line of fire that set his blood boiling.

Taking her head in his hands, he tilted her face until their mouths met. His fingers fumbled with the buckle and fastenings on his trousers.

Her hands sought out his member, gently gripping it and slowly pumping in a firm hold. Kelvaras' lifted his head and sighed, allowing the sensations to curl and twist inside him. Warmth enveloped his penis and a moan stuck in his throat as he realised that she'd taken him into her mouth. It was the nearest sensation to being inside her, moist, hot, liquid. She hungrily lapped, suckled and purred around his cock.

He didn't want to, but he eased himself out of her inviting mouth. Her skirts were the only hindrance now, and Vyvica knelt on the bed to remove the dress, the skirt pooling around her knees, revealing her long muscular legs. She kicked off the skirt one leg at a time. His fingers eased up under the edging of her underwear on either side of her hips and pulled it down.

He admired the small thatch of curls at the apex of her thighs and the dampness coming from between her legs. He held her gaze as he lowered her onto her back on the bed. His fingers explored her, his gaze holding her as her eyelids fluttered shut, small mewling noises issuing from her throat. Her musky scent wrapped around them, and he sighed. She shuddered and groaned, lacing her fingers through his hair.

He toyed with her, making her gasp and shake violently, her fingers tightened around his scalp.

For several minutes, he focused on her, listening for her fast breathing, feeling her muscles contract tighter. He kissed her once more before removing his fingers, connecting his gaze once more with hers. If it were possible, they were more liquid than before, a brilliant whiskey colour, fire dancing within them. He kept eye contact as he knelt over her.

She reached up and grasped his bare butt cheeks, trying to pull him into her. He smiled at her attempt, but held out, so the tip sat just inside her entrance.

"Kelvaras," she growled, her voice low and deep. He pushed into her, hard. She bucked beneath him, her head falling back, her black hair fanning out behind her as she struggled to breathe. Her muscles clenched around him. He pulled out and plunged in again, and once more, taking her further into the abyss. His own release was right on the brink. Every time she tightened, gasped or called out, made him edge closer, until he felt her orgasm start, her voice hoarse as she cried out. He quickened his pace, and his own orgasm ruptured, causing him to collapse against her in shuddering ecstasy.

He wrapped his arms around her and rolled onto his side, tucking her back into the curve of his stomach.

Where would he be without this woman by his side?

They lay quietly together, drifting in and out of the post coital haze that surrounded them.

CHAPTER THIRTY-THREE

"Vyvica," he sighed.

"That's commander to you," she said quietly. He felt her face stretch against his chest and looked down to find her still flushed, but smiling brightly. He kissed her forehead.

"*Commander.* You have to trust me." He felt her stiffen.

"It makes me suspicious when you say that. Why should I?"

"Some things are going to happen that you're going to think are strange, but you have to believe me, and trust me."

Vyvica pushed against him, pulling out of his arms, a hurt look on her face.

"Why can't you tell me what's going on?"

"For your own protection, Your Highness."

Vyvica closed her eyes and he realised he'd hit a nerve. He hated hurting her, but he couldn't tell her anything.

"I never wanted to be ruler of this planet. And now, I'm being used by you and Ch'ar. Are you planning on marrying me so that I'll sign the treaty?"

Kelvaras raised himself to sit on the edge of the bed, trying to find the right words.

"I'm not stupid, Kelvaras. You come in here and seduce me, try to woo me with your notion of romance, yet it's with terms and conditions. Well, I have some of my own.

"You won't have the authority to sign a treaty on my behalf if we get married. And I certainly won't be giving Ch'ar any of the planet's voting rights at the Intergalactic Senate. To be honest, I don't really want to marry you if you're only doing this to make peace with your father."

"I'm not trying to make peace with my father, I'm trying to save you!"

"You have a funny way of showing it," Vyvica hissed at him. She crawled off the bed, tugging one of the sheets over her body. "You might be trying to save me, but what deal have you made with Ch'ar?"

"I haven't made any deals. You're not being rational, Vyvica."

She laughed. "Rational? You want to discuss being rational with me? I don't think so. You don't do anything without something being in it for you. Please tell *your father* that I'm woman enough to face execution whenever he sees fit."

"Vyvica."

"It's Commander!" she hissed, turning her back on him. He quietly eased himself off the bed, and pulled his trousers back on. He heard her sniff as he tugged his shirt back over his head. Walking over, he placed his hands on her shoulders, but she shrugged him off.

"Get lost," she muttered.

Kelvaras held up his hands and backed out of the room.

"Your choice. What I get out of it is you, because that is what I want." He injected as much coldness into his voice as he could and slammed the door as he left. He leaned on the frame and wondered what had gone wrong. How had the conversation ended up being about her death, and not about their marriage?

"Pig-headed woman," he muttered.

CHAPTER THIRTY-FOUR

She didn't want to think, it was too dangerous to think.

It'd been two days since she'd seen Kelvaras. Vyvica exercised and stretched; anything to keep her mind from thinking about the inevitable.

But the moment had come. And she couldn't ignore it anymore.

Two female servants were in her room when she awoke. Both women were unfamiliar, obviously not from the previous staff. Their hangdog expressions were depressing. Vyvica attempted to talk to them, asking them what was planned for her execution, but they only grunted so she didn't bother to try again, instead accepting their ministrations.

They spent time washing her in a bath, which she thought seemed a little odd. When the two women dressed her in a rather lavish red floor length dress, she shook her head. It seemed inappropriate for an execution. There were no underskirts or petticoats, just the red silky fabric which clung to her curves. A jacket, with buckles down the front, finished off the top.

Butterflies flitted through her stomach and she took a deep breath to try and calm the shaking in her hands as she laced up her fur-lined boots. Her knees were weak as the moment drew nearer, and she wondered whether she would be able to walk on her own, or if she'd need assistance. Walking to her own execution was her preference; it would look pathetic if she needed to be carried.

The hour arrived and two guards entered her room, both wearing visors, so she couldn't tell if they were sympathetic or not. She wrung her hands as she looked at each of them.

This is it.

She stood up and allowed them to escort her from the room. They set a brisk pace as they walked through the labyrinth of passageways until they reached the throne room.

"Can we please slow down," she asked, her head spinning. She braced herself on one of the guards as he stopped and turned towards her. He shook her arm off and pushed her forward.

By the time she'd arrived, her pulse raced and sweat beaded on her forehead. She hesitated at the open door; a swarm of people stood in front of her. Overwhelmed, a wave of heat swept over her, flushing her cheeks and her knees threatened to buckle as she thought of all these people here, just to witness her death.

This isn't an execution, it's a public humiliation.

Trying to breathe became difficult; each breath struggled to relieve the crushing sensation in her chest. She'd hoped it would be a quiet affair.

Her body quivered, and cold hard fear built within her, settling in a hard lump in her stomach. The crowd parted and people clapped as she walked through. The heat from her cheeks flowed down her neck and onto her chest.

That's an unusual reaction for a death?

Surely?

At the front of the room, on the steps of the dais stood Kelvaras, smartly decked out in tight leather pants, a white shirt and a vest that matched the colour of her dress.

Her heart quickened as it dawned on her. A smile pulled at the corner of her lips as she stared at the broad smile across his face.

At least he was familiar. As she reached the dais, he held out his hand. Her fingers trembled as she trusted him with hers.

"See, I told you to trust me," he whispered into her ear. She took the opportunity to look around the room.

Ch'ar stood right behind Kelvaras, a deep frown furrowing his forehead. That fact made her happier with the marriage. The remainder of the crowd was a who's who of the Intergalactic Senate. Several of the important Royalties and Governors from around the Galaxy were in attendance. Many faces she recognised, she smiled or nodded as they acknowledged her.

"I don't see how I can trust you. I guess we're getting married?" she hissed at him.

"Too right!" he whispered back.

A tall thin man stood in front of them. She didn't recognise him, but he wore the insignia of the Senate. She cast a sideways glance at Kelvaras.

"Just to be sure it's done properly."

Vyvica couldn't resist the urge to smile.

The minister cleared his throat, looking from Kelvaras to Vyvica. Kelvaras gripped her hand tightly, his thumb brushing over her knuckles the only indication of his nerves. She found comfort in the simple action and the warmth of his grasp.

"We have come together to witness the joining of this man and this woman in the union of marriage."

"Why should I go through with this?" Vyvica whispered.

"Because you know you want to." He smiled at her, but she could tell he was nervous.

Silence filled the room and Vyvica turned towards the minister, who frowned at them.

"Sorry, please continue." She smiled sweetly.

"Is there a problem?"

"No, no problem."

"Are you sure?"

Vyvica nodded, trying to hide the relief and the sense of peace that flooded through her. The butterflies in her stomach still fluttered, but she didn't feel sick, instead it was a contented feeling.

The voice of the minister droned on, until he cleared his throat again, and Kelvaras prodded her.

"Sorry?"

The minister sighed. "Do you accept this man as your husband?" He enunciated.

Vyvica looked at Kelvaras. His eyebrows drew together, and the thumb action increased. His eyes widened a little. She was surprised to see him worried.

"I don't really have a choice."

"Are you saying that you're marrying against your will?" The minister sounded shocked.

"Yes and no. It's this or death." Nothing like creating a stir. Kelvaras' face paled, but she winked at him.

A surge of noise rippled through the crowd.

"Vyvica, think about it," Kelvaras whispered to her. Reaching up her hand, she gently cupped the side of his face. Something deep within her stirred, a feeling that she hadn't felt before.

"Excuse me," a voice from the room sounded above the hubbub. The attention of the room turned to the tall female, who moved to the front of the room. She sidled up to Vyvica.

"Greetings, Madame Head of the Senate." Vyvica bowed to her.

"Vyvica," was the curt reply. The woman, her long, red hair braided, some wrapped into a bun at the back of her head, a thick plait coming over her shoulder. Her eyes pierced into Vyvica's soul, but she knew the woman, knew what she was trying to do.

"First of all, are you Vyvica Karala, princess of Elador?"

"Yes Madame Waye, you know who I am."

"Can you verify it?" She asked.

Vyvica hadn't expected that. The woman continued to stare at her hard. She sighed, and removed the jacket, and pulling the collar off her left hand shoulder to reveal the royal birth mark." She stood silently as Madame Waye inspected it.

"Hmm." She said, pulling the top back up and indicating for Vyvica to put the jacket back on.

"Are you marrying against your will, Vyvica?"

Vyvica looked from the woman to Kelvaras. He still held one of her hands. He swallowed visibly as she looked at him, his eyes fixed on the tall imposing woman. Vyvica had to hide the smile that threatened to come over her face. Madame Waye was imposing, the reason she had been voted as the head of the Intergalactic Senate. She was a fair woman, and she didn't take kindly to any acts of unkindness, especially to woman.

"I'm marrying..." She couldn't articulate the words in her head, they were tumbling over each other.

Everyone in the room was watching in silence, waiting for a sensational response that would blow this party apart. Vyvica didn't want to give them any reason to start rioting, considering most of those who attended were obviously there to support Ch'ar. Madame Waye was the only exception.

"Vyvica, let me warn you, that this matter is to be taken seriously, I'm not going to let this marriage proceed if you are unhappy with the situation in any way."

Vyvica glanced back at Kelvaras, within her chest, her own heart, warmth flooded out, filling her veins.

This man was doing what he could to save her life.

Why would he do that?

Because he loves me, the thought rippled through her mind.

Kelvaras gripped her hand, like he was holding onto life itself. Perhaps he had put more on the line than her life.

"You love me?" The words tumbled out.

"Yes, I love you."

Noise erupted in the room once more, louder this time, but it faded to a buzz in Vyvica's ears. She inhaled sharply, the air punched from her lungs. Her legs turned to jelly and Kelvaras reached out to grab her before she fell to her knees on the dais. Her focus sharpened in on Kelvaras' face, full of concern for her. She was aware that Madame Waye was fussing at her side, but she brushed her off.

"Vyvica! Vyvica! Talk to me!" Madame Waye yelled.

"Don't yell at me," she whispered back. She shook her head, trying to clear the ringing from her ears. Her body felt hot, but in a good way.

Kelvaras knelt down, his knees touching hers. Fire seemed to come from his touch, and she longed for him to take her in his arms and kiss her, like he had two days ago. Looking deep into his eyes, she could see his genuine feelings. His hopes...dreams...their future...

"I'm alright, just...shocked."

Kelvaras let out a sigh and a nervous laugh. "Thank goodness."

She turned to Madame Waye and smiled. "I'm happy, Madame, I am. Just shocked."

"If you are being coerced into this marriage, I need to know. The senate needs to know. You are the crown princesses, and I'm not sure why your father isn't here to officiate this, but I need to know that you are consenting to this marriage without duress."

Ch'ar pushed his way into the group, grabbing Vyvica by the arm, pinching into her bicep. Madame Waye glared at him.

"Unhand her now, or the wedding will not proceed." Ch'ar tried to outstare the woman, but he backed off.

The noise around them subsided, and the minister knelt down between them.

"Do you want to proceed?"

All eyes were on her, and Vyvica heard every single breathe being held. She looked at Kelvaras, hope in his face. She reached out her hand and took his once more.

"Yes, I want to go ahead." She turned to Madame Waye. "I consent to this marriage. This is the man I want to spend my life with." Kelvaras blew his breath out, hitting her face, but she smiled at him.

"Thank you," he mouthed to her before the minister called the room to order, and once the simmering conversation quietened down enough, he glanced at Vyvica. She smiled, holding tightly onto Kelvaras' hand and nodded. The minister cleared his throat. He stared down at them, indicating for them to stand. She couldn't help but giggle as they got to their feet. The minister waited a moment for Ch'ar and Madame Waye to move aside before continuing.

"If there is any legal reason why these two should not join together, bring forth the information now."

A tense silence followed, filled with the sound of fabric moving as everyone anxiously looked around, many glances flitting to Madame Waye, whose stern face continued to study Vyvica. She smiled at the older woman, pleased that someone at least cared enough to stop the wedding if she felt it was necessary, but Vyvica had made up her mind.

The minister nodded, satisfied and proceeded once more.

"Kelvaras Mason and Vyvica Karala D'Authian, you have agreed to this union?"

They both verbally consented. Vyvica's heartrate increased with each breath, waiting for the minister to allow them to kiss, allowing her to finally be able to touch Kelvaras as his wife.

"You have agreed to this union in front of the assembly, you are therefore considered husband and wife." Kelvaras let go of her hand and hooked his arms over her shoulders, pulling her towards him. He leaned down to her, a smile on his lips and in his eyes.

Her heart fluttered with anticipation.

CHAPTER THIRTY-FIVE

"My beloved," he whispered across her lips as they touched hers with electrifying results. The ground rumbled and shook underneath their feet.

She broke off the kiss as ice showered down on them, and the gasps of surprise from the audience broke through her bubble of happiness.

"Right on cue." Kelvaras smiled, pulling Vyvica under his arm and rushing her from the room.

"What's going on?"

"Remember how I said 'trust me'? That's Tyron and the D'Authian guards."

"What?"

"I orchestrated for them to arrive *after* the wedding ceremony, what better way to create a diversion?"

Another explosion, a lot closer this time, the ground swelling upward underneath them. Some of the guests screamed, as others scrambled for the doorway.

Vyvica couldn't speak, she didn't trust herself to. She wanted to say something smart and sassy, but his forward thinking had been clever.

"Where're we going?" she asked as Kelvaras rushed her down the corridors.

"Back to your room."

"But"—" Vyvica tried to stop him, but the long fabric of her skirt kept tripping her up.

"I'm taking you back there so you can get changed, Commander! Do you want your troops seeing you in a dress?" A frown creased between her eyes. "I mean, it's absolutely stunning, and I love the way it shows off all your curves, but it's completely impractical for fighting in." He grinned at her. She couldn't help but grin back as they reached her room, only to find the walls punched out and Tyron standing in the ruins, a bag under his arm.

"Commander, pleased to see you're well."

"You were in on this whole marriage thing?"

Tyron tilted his head as she ran to him and embraced him.

"We need to get you ready for battle, we need our commander." He smiled as he thrust the bag towards her. She pulled the contents out and pulled the pants on underneath the skirt of her dress. Unlacing the bodice, she let it slide down her body. She pulled her thermal top on and grabbed her leather jacket. Her fingers lingered on the smooth fabric of her wedding dress. She rolled it up and stashed it back within her bag, hoping it would keep it safe until she could return for it. She pushed the bag under the bed and exhaled loudly.

"Much better. Now, where are my weapons?"

Kelvaras handed her a laser pistol and she cocked it, hearing the mechanism fire up to a whine inside the machine.

"Now I feel human again, let's get this started." Tyron handed her a communicator which she strapped to her wrist.

"Ready, Commander?" Another voice interrupted her. A familiar face appeared behind Tyron, his weapon held aloft.

Brett.

Vyvica grinned at him as she switched on her communicator.

"Everyone listening?" She transmitted. There were a few cheers before various voices responded.

"Right, Tyron, the guests will have spread out throughout the castle, escaping from the firefight, can you round up the visitors and dignitaries and get them back on their vessels. We will herd Ch'ar's men into the throne room.

Brett, you go down to the basement. Kelvaras, you stay on this level and push the men into the throne room. I'll take the top floor and we'll push down.

"I need a third of you on the basement floor with Brett; a third with Kelvaras, a third with me. Understood?"

An explosion ripped through the ground beneath them, and the floor rocked violently.

"Go." Vyvica didn't wait for any responses as she yelled into the communicator. Her team didn't either. She clicked the safety off on her weapon.

"Take care, Commander." Tyron hugged her again, before he and Brett ran off down the corridor. Vyvica looked up at Kelvaras, her heart pounding, and it wasn't all because of him. The thought of battle filled her with adrenaline and she was ready for the fight.

"Come back in one piece, Commander," Kelvaras said as Vyvica walked up to him.

"That's Vyvica, to you." She smiled, raking her hand over his short hair, and pulling his head down. She kissed him deeply, not wanting it to end.

"Love you," he murmured as he ran off down the corridor. He turned and looked back before he turned the corner. His face light, warmth flowing from his gaze.

A laser blast lit up the hall behind her, and she pivoted on her heels to fire a volley of shots down the corridor.

"Friendly fire, Commander," came a call, and she lowered her weapon as her own troops came around the corner to meet her. She smiled broadly at the men and women.

"Let's get Elador back!" A chorus of cheers answered her call and she ran the opposite way to which Kelvaras had gone.

CHAPTER THIRTY-SIX

The entire city was in disarray. Each explosion reminded her of when she'd left, when she'd abandoned her father. The guilt of leaving him at the time crushed her and still did; especially now she knew he was dead. Ch'ar hadn't told her how he'd died, and she didn't want to know.

An explosion ripped through the wall beside her, bringing her back to the present, as she ducked and ran past, dodging the debris that smashed against the opposite wall and showered her body in ice particles. The leather jacket afforded some protection, but her face and hands bled as ice shards embedded into her skin.

The guards ran towards the throne room, herding Ch'ar's army in, where they would be detained.

The army threw their weapons into a pile outside the door as they entered the large room. Tyron stood to one side, and approached Vyvica as she entered.

"Are the Senators safe?"

"Yes, they are all on their vessels and being sent to Apos as we speak."

"Why Apos? Why not send them back to their home planets?"

"They wanted to witness the return of the D'Authian Dynasty to the throne," Tyron said with a triumphant smile. Vyvica didn't feel the same gratitude that he did.

The floor underneath them quaked and Vyvica held herself upright in the door frame.

"Have you seen or heard from Kelvaras?" she asked. Her own communicator had been noisy with chatter from the other levels, but she hadn't heard from Kelvaras himself. Her eyebrows drew down and she chewed on her bottom lip as she waited for Tyron's response.

"No, Commander, I haven't heard anything."

"I'm going to have a look around."

"Be careful, Commander."

She didn't focus on his words as she ran out the door and straight into Brett.

"Sorry, Commander."

"Come with me," she yelled at him as she ran past him.

"Commander?"

"We're going to find Kelvaras."

CHAPTER THIRTY-SEVEN

Kelvaras and his men pushed the last lot of men down the hallway towards the throne room. He hadn't seen Ch'ar in his travels, and he was determined to bring him in. There was no way he would let him escape.

"Anyone seen Ch'ar?" he asked. Ch'ar's own men hadn't and no one from the D'Authian Guard had.

"Where did Ch'ar go?" he asked one of the men he'd seen with Ch'ar.

"I don't know. I haven't seen him," the man sneered at him.

Kelvaras shrugged. How would he know where to start looking for him? He ran back out into the corridor, hoping that Ch'ar had gone to his own quarters, which were on this level. He ran down the maze of corridors, missing out most of the action, as men ran past him towards the chaos.

He located Ch'ar's quarters, but he wasn't there. He sighed as he looked around, raking a hand over his head.

Where would he have gone?

A noise attracted his attention, swearing and clanging as something heavy and metal hit the floor. He ran into an office to find Ch'ar pulling documents roughly into a case.

"Could use a hand, son."

"Don't call me that," Kelvaras hissed. Ch'ar turned and stared at him.

"Are you denying who you are?"

"I might be your son, but I don't have to accept you as my father."

"No, but you're now the King of Althu, I need you, Kelvaras."

"You don't need me, besides, I'm not going with you."

"Yes, you are. A bomb is going to go off in a matter of minutes. I need you as living proof that the D'Authian Dynasty survived."

"You can't do that." Panic welled up in Kelvaras' chest. He started to back away from Ch'ar. He had to tell the others.

"Don't tell me what to do. Here, take this." Ch'ar pushed a metal case into Kelvaras' arms. He refused to take it, so with a sigh, Ch'ar dumped it at his feet. He grabbed Kelvaras by his collar and forced him against the wall.

"You *will* take that. You *are* coming with me, whether you like it or not."

Kelvaras tried to swallow, his throat closing with the pressure of Ch'ar's grip on it. He shook his head, indicating his disproval. The pressure increased and black spots appeared in his vision.

"Don't make this harder on yourself. I need you, you need me. Besides, they will see you with me, and know that you double crossed them." Kelvaras continued to shake his head, Ch'ar's image darkening as he gasped for air.

"Your choice." More pressure was applied and he thought his head would explode.

Just one more gasp of air!

Please!

He tried to convey to his father, his eyes swollen and bulging, but Ch'ar continued to hold his airway closed.

His body relaxed.

The last thing he remembered was the nasty smile on his father's face, as his vision shrank down to a pinpoint of light, extinguishing quickly.

CHAPTER THIRTY-EIGHT

Vyvica and Brett ran down the corridor, encountering many of their own men and women as they went.

"Commander?"

Vyvica skidded to a halt and looked around. She stared at the dark haired woman who had called to her.

"Commander, we've rounded up Ch'ar's men here, but our men seem to be having trouble down in the docking bay."

"Thank you. Have you seen Kelvaras?" she asked.

Soft brown hair shook around her face as the woman responded. Trepidation seized Vyvica's chest. No one had seen or heard from Kelvaras since she'd sent him off.

"We'll go to the docking bay," she called as she headed in that direction.

Running through the hallways had brought vague directions and areas back to her mind. She was fairly certain that if she kept following this corridor, it would come out onto the top deck of the docking bay, a large open plan, two storied bay where vessels parked, refuelled and mechanical work was done on them. Brett's footsteps dogged hers as she came to a door with a portal and rather than rushing through she peered into the port below.

A fire fight kept their men contained at various lower floor entrances, laser fire crisscrossed the room ricocheting off various pods and machinery. Neither side had the upper hand but her men appeared to be well covered. The only bodies she saw looked to be Ch'ar's men, which encouraged her.

Vyvica looked across the roof space. Heavy beams and steel framing stretched across the span. She looked at Brett and could see he was thinking the same thing.

"It's risky," he said. Vyvica lifted her top lip in a snarl. Brett couldn't help but laugh. "Stating the obvious again, sorry. Do you think we can get across?"

"We could, but can we do it quietly enough?" They both looked at the span of the room; the other side provided no cover for them. They would have to act fast if they didn't want to be killed.

"Of course we can." She rewarded him with a smile.

Vyvica tapped her earpiece communicator. "Lieutenant, can you hear me?"

"Loud and clear, Commander."

"We're directly above you, are you able to give us covering fire?"

"What do you plan to do?"

Vyvica ground her teeth, she didn't like having her orders questioned. "Not over open comms. Just give us covering fire, all right?"

"Yes, Commander."

She waited and saw an increase in fire from beneath them. Quietly as they could, Brett opened the door, allowing Vyvica entrance onto the metal platform. A stairway twisted down to the left, but that wasn't what Vyvica was interested in. She climbed onto the handrail surrounding the platform, and pulled herself up onto the ceiling beam, wide enough for her to stand on. Slowly, she inched forward to allow Brett to climb as well. He didn't have her arm strength and scrambled to reach the beam. Once up, they waited. The laser fire kept up at a consistent rate.

Vyvica ran as fast as she dared, then launched herself over to the steel scaffolding, grabbing with her hands and swinging her legs until she pitched herself forward and landed on a narrow ledge above a group of Ch'ar's guards. The noise of the laser fire had distracted Ch'ar's men and covered the noise of her landing. None of them looked up.

She glanced over at Brett, who looked awkward. He didn't have the gymnastic skills she did, and she suddenly felt very vulnerable. Crouching down, she closed her eyes, willing him to land quietly, but knew that it wouldn't work like that. She opened her eyes and saw him kneeling on the scaffolding beside her. She breathed out and smiled at him.

He smiled back, relief etched on his face.

Standing above the men, they counted ten of them. Another twenty hung back underneath the beam, but where they stood, Vyvica and Brett were protected from their direct line of fire.

"What now?" Brett moved in close to Vyvica, whispering into her ear so the noise didn't carry.

"Drop in and say hello."

"That's a twenty foot drop!"

"And a soft landing," she replied as she stood up. She tucked her weapon into her side and put her feet together, slipping down silently between two support posts. Wind pushed her hair back as she fell swiftly and, in one smooth motion, she landed on a box above the men, pulling her weapon out. The startled men turned around.

"I'll blow the head off the first man that fires," she said. They dropped their weapons and raised their hands in surrender. The door opposite them opened, with more of her troops swarming into the space. Two ran to approach her.

"Cover this group, while I take care of the others," she called out. "Come on, Brett." She looked up and watched as he lowered himself down, his arms straining to hold his weight.

"Easy target," she hissed as he swung his legs and let go, executing a clumsy flip in the air before landing on the hard ice floor below her, weapon in hand. One eyebrow raised as she watched him, impressed that he'd been training. Brett smiled back, nodding, as if reading her mind.

The remainder of Ch'ar's men were boxed in, Vyvica saw a head rise up and then a weapon appeared from behind a mechanical lift and benches pushed over for protection. The weapon fired. She pushed Brett one way and used the momentum to force herself in the opposite direction. The blast hit the floor and ice splintered into the air. Vyvica rolled to her feet looking for Brett. His eyes were wide with shock and fear. She gestured to him, trying to tell him that she was going around the back, and he was to try and draw any fire his way. The head popped back over the top, but Brett fired above it, making it bob back down again.

Vyvica nodded and crept around the back, keeping her movements to a minimum. Crates were mounted up at the back, too high for her to jump and climb up. She looked around the small area, but there was nothing to climb up on.

A small lifting pod sat in the corner. On quiet feet, she ran to it and sat on the small padded seat. It rumbled quietly, having been left on. She moved it over to the crates and manoeuvred it over to the lowest one. Putting the forks under the crate, she looked around. A rope sat discarded in the corner. She tied the rope to the controller and set it into the lift position. Hopping off the seat she ran to the side, hoping that the other crates wouldn't fall on her, and waited.

The small machine lifted three heavy crates. She heard cries of surprise as the crates slowly tilted over towards the men. She fired her laser underneath the small gap between the crates and heard screams as the laser hit someone. Yells and chaos ensued as the crates fell into the gap and several men were crushed.

Others rushed out, dropping their guns and putting their hands in the air. More of her people came scrambling around the corner, keeping their lasers on the new captives. Vyvica searched around, hoping that was all of them, but a flickering light caught her attention. She approached it cautiously.

"Damn!" she said as she realised what it was. Brett ran up beside her and swore as he recognised it too. A bomb big enough to blow a dent in the planet the size of the city.

"Tyron, we have a situation in the docking bay, its *urgent!*"

"On my way."

No hesitation, relief coursed through her. He would know what to do.

The small black box emitted red and yellow flashing lights on the front. There didn't appear to be an external timer, so they didn't know how long they had until it exploded, blowing up everyone and everything within the City walls.

A hand clamped on her shoulder and she turned to see Tyron looking down at her.

"It's best we evacuate."

"I'm not losing my home again," she replied, tears in her eyes. She stared at Tyron, hoping the intensity of her feelings were enough to make him aware that now she had won her home back, she wasn't going to give it up now.

"We don't know how long we have."

"Can't you defuse it?"

"It's too dangerous, child." He slipped his arm around her shoulders trying to pull her away. She cringed at the term 'child'. She wasn't one anymore, hadn't been for several years.

"Kelvaras," she breathed, her eyes widened. "I have to find him."

"Haven't you heard from him?"

"No."

Tyron cursed as he looked back at the black box.

"I'll see what I can do here," he said, sighing.

"Thank you!" Vyvica threw her arms around him and hugged him before turning on her heel.

"Commander?" Vyvica looked back at who spoke to her. A dark curly headed woman, the worried look on her face made Vyvica's heart freeze in her chest.

"Yes"?"

"I saw Kelvaras on the top deck, he was being supported by Ch'ar. I think they're heading for the docking port on the roof. Commander, it didn't look good. From where I was, Kelvaras looked like he was going voluntarily with Ch'ar."

Vyvica breathed in sharply. Emotions whirled around inside of her, but she kept her face calm.

"The roof? Brett, let's go."

Vyvica raced through the docking port, crashing through the doors, not waiting to hear if Brett followed her or not. She had to get to Kelvaras to see for herself whether he was defecting or not. Her heart skipped beats as she thought about him leaving.

Although they were married, he wouldn't be able to sign the treaty agreement, but that wouldn't stop Ch'ar from trying. She didn't want to think that Kelvaras would do that.

Would he?

She remembered the warmth in his eyes. "Trust me," he'd said. She swallowed the lump in her throat.

She would have to.

CHAPTER THIRTY-NINE

The passenger pod blasters were on idle, the heat intense as Vyvica and Brett ran onto the launching platform.

"Damn!" Vyvica yelled as she watched the pod laboriously lift off. It gained a little height before Brett pointed to the left. The mooring line was still attached. Vyvica smiled.

"Can we pull that thing in?" She yelled over the noise of the blasters.

"Not without mechanical help."

Hopelessness flittered into her chest and settled around her heart as the pod blasters fired into gear and the pod shot forward, only to be restrained by the mooring line. The line pinged taut, held, and snapped back, pulling the vessel with it. The pod crashed onto the edge of the building, sending chunks of rock and metal flying and the building rocked and vibrated underneath them. Vyvica and Brett ducked, protecting their heads with their arms.

The pod perched precariously on the end of the building and Vyvica held her breath as it pitched forward and fell in slow motion.

"No!" She screamed leaping forward. Brett caught her around the waist and held her.

"It's not safe, Commander." The sound of wrenching and twisting metal rang out in her ears. One of the landing legs caught on the lip of the building and held it there.

"Brett, tie that leg off. I'm going in." Thinking on her feet, Vyvica went to the edge of the building and looked down at the pod.

"But Commander"—""

"That's an order," she snapped, desperately looking for a way to enter the pod. Glancing over the side of the building, she watched the pod sway against the ice walls, two blasters spluttered, the third still fired on full. The only way into the transporter pod was through the passenger door, and she would probably have to pry that open.

Her mind raced as she watched Brett tie another two mooring ropes around the leg, securing it as best he could.

"Is there any more rope?" she asked. Brett looked around and grabbed a long length.

"Perfect." She tied it around her middle and gave him the end. "Give me some slack to work with, but if the vessel goes, hold on for your life."

"Commander"—""

"I'm going to try and get into the passenger side door, once in there I will know where he is. Hopefully we can make it out together."

Brett paled, but nodded. "Yes, commander"."

With her heart pounding loudly in her ears, she eased herself over the building and onto the side of the pod.

"Let me down slow until I yell, OK?"

"Yes, Commander."

Vyvica pushed herself away from the pod, abseiling down a way.

"Stop!" She called out as she came to the pod door. As she predicted, the angle of the pod would not allow for the door to open manually, she would have to pry it. The knife on her belt should do the trick. She manoeuvred the blade underneath the electronic pad and twisted. It popped the panel up, short circuiting the door, making the seal release. With the knife planted firmly in the doorway, Vyvica used her body weight to wedge it open, wide enough for her to look inside.

The open cabin contained a jumble of seats and debris which had flown around when the vessel crashed, but no people.

The hatch to the pilot's cabin was closed. Ch'ar must have Kelvaras there. She clambered through the door and stood on the seat closest to her; a convenient set of stairs.

She tugged on the rope and was given more slack.

CHAPTER FORTY

Kelvaras opened his eyes and stared at the ground looming before him.

He yelped in fear.

Where the hell am I?

The last thing he remembered was...

"Ch'ar!" He looked around as he spoke. Ch'ar lay on the windscreen of the vessel, stirring.

"What the hell happened?" he yelled at the man. Ch'ar lifted his head, and as he did, a line splintered out across the glass. The thick atmospheric windshield cracked.

"How the hell should I know?" Ch'ar fired back at him.

Blood pumped into 'Kelvaras' head, making his temples pound. He knew that they were in a precarious situation, but it wasn't until he looked down he realised he was strapped to the seat. His arms hung at a strange angle. The whole front of the vessel pointed at the ground, and the groaning and shrieking of the metal around him made him aware that he didn't have a lot of time before the transporter pod would plummet.

If he undid his strap, he would tumble onto the screen and might give the vessel the momentum it needed to continue its fall.

He had to work out what he needed to do.

Ch'ar couldn't lift himself off the windscreen. Every time he moved, a cracking sound echoed through the cockpit, making them both aware that time was short.

He had to escape.

Kelvaras turned to investigate the seat which remained firmly fixed to the floor, and if he stood on it, he would be able to open the hatch into the main passenger cabin and climb out. But what kind of mess would there be behind the door? Would he be able to get out of the cabin?

"Too many questions," he muttered. If he let the strap go and held on, he might be able to swing himself up onto the chair. If not, he would end up with Ch'ar. He reached a hand behind him and tried to take his weight on one arm. It felt awkward and put strain on his tricep muscle, but he was confident he could do it. With his other hand, he reached over and pushed on the latch to the belt.

As the belt released, he grabbed onto the chair before he dropped down. His body swung, and his arms tensed, but he held on. Slowly he pulled himself up onto the seat, feeling it give a little underneath him. Adrenaline coursed through his veins.

He didn't really care what happened, as long as he *tried* to get out.

The hatch above him opened.

He glanced at the face that peeked through and smiled up at the brilliant face of his bride.

"Thank goodness you're here," he said, reaching out towards her. She grabbed his hand and with the help of her pull, he swung his legs up, and gained purchase on the side of the door.

"Where are you going?" Ch'ar shouted.

"I'm going to be with my wife," Kelvaras spat back. He looked down at the man trying to stand on the windscreen. Ch'ar's face was red and twisted in fury.

Vyvica pulled him through the hatch and threw her arms around him. Safe at last, he allowed himself to be hugged.

A laser blast echoed in the confined chamber and Kelvaras felt a searing pain in his side. Fire burned within his chest. The acrid smell of burnt leather and hair filled his nose, along with a slightly sweet smell of his bride. He smiled at Vyvica.

"No!" He heard as his vision blacked out. She squeezed him tight, pulling him towards the wall that she stood on, but everything grew quieter. He slumped forward, aware of hands and frantic movement around him.

CHAPTER FORTY-ONE

Kelvaras lay on top of her, his breathing ragged and loud in her ears.

"Kelvaras! Are you listening to me? Damn it, listen!"

No response.

Tears stung her eyes as she held him. A laugh from the cabin below brought her back to reality and Ch'ar.

He had done this.

She was going to end it.

Even if it meant her life.

She would take him down with her.

Gently, she pushed Kelvaras until he leaned on the wall and edged past him to look into the cabin. Ch'ar had managed to gain his feet and stood on the screen, his laser in his hand. He chuckled as she looked down at him.

"Can't have a happily ever after now, can we?"

Anger surged through her, an anger she had never known before.

Her vision flushed red and white as she looked at the man she hated.

"There won't be for you," she said as she threw her knife down at him. He dodged to one side and it landed with a clatter on the windshield. A tiny crack opened underneath it.

"That was rather pathetic. You should've married me. I'm more of a man than he'll ever be. We could have ruled this planet, an alliance. Instead you had to marry him."

"He's your son!" Shocked at the words, she grimaced as he spoke. Her loyalties lay with the man dying beside her.

"Ha! Son in name only! He never looked at me as his father and I wasn't there for him, so I didn't expect anything from him, and I wasn't disappointed. Neither was he."

Vyvica looked around for something else to throw, but couldn't see anything heavy enough to break the shield. She looked at Kelvaras who lay on his side, still breathing, his face pale, lips turning an unusual shade.

She had to act fast.

Looking around the cabin revealed no weapons, not that there would be on an intergalactic passenger pod. On Kelvaras' belt she glimpsed his laser gun. She smiled as she bent forward to kiss his lips.

"Thank you, sweetheart." She unhooked the weapon and looked back into the cabin. Ch'ar remained stranded on the screen. The pilot's and copilot's chair out of his reach.

"Your son said thank you." She smiled sweetly. "And see you in hell." She gritted her teeth and snarled as she levelled her weapon at the screen and fired. The shield absorbed the laser, but cracks spider-webbed out and splintered with the weight on it.

"No!" screeched Ch'ar as the screen creaked and snapped, and smashed into thousands of pieces. With his arms cartwheeling, a hand gripped onto an undamaged section of screen.

Blood poured from cuts on his hands, making his grasp slippery.

"Vyvica! Help me!" His voice high pitched with fear and pleading, his face white, eyes large with fear. He changed grip as his fingers slipped, his legs scrambling underneath him.

Vyvica watched in morbid fascination as one by one, his fingers slid off the bloody surface, and he opened his mouth.

His scream echoed around the walls of the cabin and cockpit. Ch'ar seemed to be suspended in mid-air, before he plummeted to his death.

That's one less thing to worry about.

The vessel groaned and creaked as the shield let go, and jostled up and down once the weight of Ch'ar had left. The noise of rope stretching and metal tearing galvanised Vyvica into action. With the rope still tied around her waist she wasn't going to be able to move far, or get Kelvaras out. She tugged on it, trying to get more rope.

"Are you all right?" Brett's voice mumbled through the hull of the pod.

"Yeah, can you give me more slack?" she yelled back. Rope came in through the gap, allowing her more room.

Without warning, the vessel dropped. Human screams from outside the pod told her that they now had a group of people watching or helping. Dust swirled around inside the cabin and she sneezed.

"Commander? The vessel isn't going to hold for much longer!"

"I know!" Her heart raced in her chest. She untied herself from the rope, and with difficulty, tied it around Kelvaras' waist.

Will I be able to hang onto him?

She hoped so.

"Brett! Can you pull us up?" she yelled. A faint reply, then a tugging on the rope. Slowly, Kelvaras lifted, his unconscious body bowed in the middle. That wasn't going to work.

"Stop!" She cursed as the rope lowered back down and Kelvaras lay back down on the ground.

"He's a dead weight!" she called out desperately. "He's unconscious."

"Is he dead?" another voice called out. Relief flooded through her when she heard it.

"No he isn't, Tyron, and I'm not going to let him die!" She heard chuckling from above, through the noise of stretching and twisting metal.

"I presume you defused the bomb?"

"You could say that. Tie yourself together with him, we have enough men to pull you up," Tyron shouted back.

"You hear that, Kelvaras?" she whispered to him, as she swept her hand across his clammy forehead. "The cavalry are here." She juggled him into a sitting position and, using a carabineer, clipped herself onto his belt. "Hope this works." She looked at his face, pale, his lips almost blue. "Don't give up on me now. Who else will I have to boss around?" She placed her arms around him and kissed his cold lips. Chills swept through her. He was very still.

"Ready!" she called.

The rope tugged once more, and using her body, she kept him in an upright position. She was able to assist herself up onto the chairs, using her own weight as well as those pulling to keep him moving and in a more vertical position. The rope stopped moving as the vessel shuddered and dropped beneath them. Her body weight pulled on the carabineer as the chair she stood on fell away. Panting, she struggled to find a better foothold as she heard the men above curse.

"We're all right. Keep pulling." Wrapping her legs around Kelvaras to keep him steady, she allowed the men above to pull them up. Slowly they inched their way through the pod, the metal protesting as gravity tried to pull it towards the ground.

As they came to the door, Vyvica twisted Kelvaras around, so that she could pull herself through first, then drag him through.

At that moment, the world around her erupted. The vessel dropped, she screamed as it tilted, stabilised, then fell away underneath her. She wrapped herself around Kelvaras as they were thrown into the air and against the side of the building, banging heavily on her side, the wind knocked out of her.

A large ball of fire exploded upwards from the smashed vessel.

Still out of breath, she felt the rope bite into her side as they were heaved upwards. She couldn't hear anything, only the vision of the fireball filled her view.

Slowly sound returned.

The heat forcing upwards clawed at them as hands grasped and hauled them over the edge. Intense heat and pain seared into Vyvica's feet and legs, and then she was lying on a hard cold surface, trying desperately to breathe.

She opened her eyes and looked around. Tyron beside her, smiling. Kelvaras lay, attached by remnants of the rope to her at the waist, Brett and another person attending to him. They unclipped Kelvaras and started working on him. She smiled, kissing her forefinger and placed it over Kelvaras' lips before they picked him up and bustled him off the exposed roof.

She looked around at the carnage. Smoke poured out of every open doorway and through the roof. Spasmodic weapon fire could be heard, but mostly the Crown City of Althu was surrounded by a pall of destruction.

"We did it. We won it back," Tyron said, sitting upright and pulling Vyvica with him. She clasped her head in her hands, not really focusing on his words.

"What about Kelvaras?" she whispered. Tyron held her face in his hands, using his thumbs to wipe the tears from her face.

Tyron stood and held out a hand towards her. She took it, then leaned on Tyron's shoulder, gentle sobs wracking her aching body, but she allowed the older gentleman to put his arm around her, kissing the top of her head.

CHAPTER FORTY-TWO

Kelvaras was in an induced coma for three days to give his body a chance to recover. Another week of intensive physical therapy topped off the healing. Ch'ar's weapon had ruptured a lung, narrowly missing the heart. She'd sat beside him every day while he slept and healed, allowing Tyron to take control of the clean-up.

The Crown City of Althu was a mess, but Tyron believed they would be able to rebuild it. They'd discussed plans and various options to make the Crown City more secure.Vyvica was no longer the commander of the D'Authian Guards, instead she'd been made the Regent as her father's death had been documented. It had been a tedious wait for the coronation. Now that they had the city back, and she'd fought hard for it, she realised what the city meant to her.

What the planet meant to her.

The day of the coronation arrived, six weeks after their wedding and the fateful day she thought she'd lost him.

They stood outside the throne room, and Vyvica fidgeted with the hem on the sleeve of her dress, looking down at the ground. Kelvaras put his hand under her chin, pulling her face up.

"What's wrong?"

"Nothing," she said softly.

"You're anxious, Vyvica. What are you worried about?"

He looked deep into her dark eyes, searching them. She blinked, sighed and took his hands in hers.

"I'm worried."

"Oh Vyvica, what about?"

She swallowed hard, looking away, before returning to gaze into his eyes.

"I'm nervous. I...I didn't want to be queen. I've been groomed for it all my life, but when the planet was taken, all I wanted was to get my father back, so he could rule, and I could...I don't know, do something else." She shrugged. "I didn't feel like I was capable of being a queen, or making decisions that would affect thousands of people."

Kelvaras held her at arm's length, studying her face, before pulling her into his embrace, holding her tight. "Vyvica, you'll make a great queen."

"But...what if I'm not?"

His hand smoothed her hair and it felt calming. Her shoulders dropped a little as the sound of his voice and the action of his hand in her hair soothed her.

"You managed to lead the D'Authian Guards quite well for a few years, just think of it as an extended army."

"I can't do this on my own."

"And you won't have to. I'll be right beside you. I have been for the last month, supported you with every decision you've had to make as the Regent. Vyvica, I know you can do this, between my head and your brawn, we'll work it out."

She giggled into his chest and he held her tighter, squeezing her against him. She looked up, tiptoed and kissed him on the lips.

"Thank you."

"For what?"

"For talking sense to me."

"That's what I mean, Vyvica, my brains, your brawn." She smiled again.

The door to the throne room opened and they were beckoned into the room. Kelvaras held his arm out and Vyvica linked hers through. He kissed the top of her head before they walked into the room. Applause erupted around them as they walked down the aisle to the dais where Tyron stood in full D'Authian uniform.

His eyes shone and he smiled widely as he watched Vyvica walk towards him. He kissed her when they stopped in front of him, and shook Kelvaras' hand.

"Welcome senators, governors, principalities and citizens. Thank you for coming today and witnessing the crowning of Vyvica Karala D'Authian, and Kelvaras Mason."

He turned to the two of them and smiled like a proud father.

"I've known Vyvica since she was born. She's been quite a handful, and when Kelvaras asked me if he could marry her, I said yes, please, take her off my hands." Vyvica's opened her mouth wide, feigning shock at his words. "Yes, he asked me."

She turned and gave Kelvaras' arm a lighthearted slap as the crowd tittered.

"All joking aside, this young man has brought peace, sense and stability into her life, and I'm thankful. So it is with great pleasure, and privilege, that I was asked to perform the coronation ceremony. So without further delaying, how about we start." He nodded and both of them stepped up onto the dais, Vyvica took the large throne, Kelvaras stood to her left. She reached over and sought out his left hand, her fingers trembling. The squeeze he gave reassured her, and she braved a quick glance at him, smiling her thanks.

"Vyvica Karala D'Authian, as the rightful heir to the throne, do you accept the responsibility of the position?" Tyron asked.

"Yes, I realise the full implications of the role, and I steadfastly agree to look after this planet, protect the people, and ensure that all of the decisions that affect the people are made with honesty and integrity," Vyvica replied without faltering.

Kelvaras gave her hand another squeeze before she let his go. She bowed down in front of Tyron, studying a spot on the carpet in front of his feet. It seemed like forever before she felt the delicate circlet of diamond-encrusted gold placed upon her head. She stood and smiled as the crowd cheered.

"Kelvaras Mason, do you agree to support your wife in her role as the Queen of Elador?"

"I agree to support and encourage her, give counsel to her when she needs it, and stand behind all decisions that she makes with honesty and integrity."

Vyvica watched with pride as he bowed before Tyron. The crown on his head was a thicker band of gold, and heavy. He made some comment to Tyron, and they sniggered together.

He stood up to the crowd's applause.

"Take your seats," Tyron announced.

Vyvica gathered the skirt up and sat on the large throne, before Kelvaras took his seat.

"Senators, governors, principalities and citizens. I present to you, Queen Vyvica and King Kelvaras. Long may the Queen reign."

Many cheers went up as everyone repeated the last sentence. Kelvaras turned to gaze at her, smiling as he claimed her hand again. Her face hot, as she smiled and waved at the crowd.

"I've got your back," he said to her as he kissed her cheek. The smile on her face grew wider. She kissed his cheek back before they were surrounded by well-wishers.

All formalities aside, both clasped hands, refusing to be separated as they'd to endure the function and receive well wishes from intergalactic dignitaries who had attended the coronation.

When all duties had been discharged, they'd sneaked off, stripping off their formal attire as they embraced, kissed, caressed and giggled to their bed chamber, collapsing onto the bed is a frenzy of sexual fervour.

CHAPTER FORTY-THREE

Vyvica lay beside him, watching him sleep. His eyes flickered.

He woke, and she watched the expressions flit across his face as he surfaced.

She lay still, waiting.

She watched as Kelvaras mumbled, and she leaned down to him.

"What was that?" she asked softly.

"How is the queen of my heart?" he asked, brushing his stubbly face against her forehead.

"Fine thanks, Mr...what would you prefer to be called? Mr D'Authian or Mr Karala?"

One eye popped open and stared at her.

"What's wrong with Mason?"

"Mason? You seriously don't expect me to take your name, do you?" She smirked at him as he opened his other eye.

"Is this to be our first argument?" He smiled back, pulling her on top of him.

"Maybe? I love the way we settle arguments, my lord." His eyes glazed slightly as she rested her chin on his chest. Only hours earlier they'd jointly declared to reign with honour, providing prosperity to the planet and to rule with fairness.

"Hmm, I like that. Call me 'my lord', again," he muttered. Vyvica smirked.

"As much as you like being in control?" She nipped at the skin on his neck.

He growled as he grabbed her wrists and twisted, rolling her underneath him, her arms held in one of his strong hands above her head. She shrieked and giggled as he stroked his other hand down her side, grabbing a handful of her butt cheek, squeezing it.

"You can control the planet, my dear, but in this room, in this City, I control you." He playfully bit her ear lobe.

A shiver of anticipation shot up her spine. She thrust her hips upwards, grinding them into him.

"You're a vixen aren't you," he said, nuzzling her neck, laying down kisses interspersed with bites as he made his way to her breasts.

She sighed as his tongue and teeth grazed across one of her nipples.

"I'll make a deal with you," she said huskily.

"I don't think you're in a position to make deals." He chuckled into her skin, sending thrills of desire firing through her and settling in her groin.

"I'm in control in the kingdom, and you're the boss in the bedroom."

"That's what I said."

"No, mine's different." She twisted her thighs around his, turned her body and flicked, causing him to topple off her. Using the element of surprise, she captured his hands, forcing them above his head and laying on top of him.

"I let you do that." He grinned, his eyes wide. He bucked beneath her, but her legs remained locked around his hips, containing them, and keeping him in place.

"Okay, agreed. You win," he said, lifting his head up to plant a kiss on her lips.

"Yes, I do," she said, smiling as she kissed him.

"But only for now." A wicked glint shone in his eyes.

The End

Behind the Story

There is a bit of a story behind Shards of Ice. It is a sad tale, one where I lost three years in the quagmire of life.

Shards of Ice was based on a dream I had back in 2007, a great idea that needed a little work. Basically I saw thousands of vessels fleeing from an underground garage, each containing a female. I developed the story, with the idea that Vyvica would be able to talk to her father who remained a prisoner in Althu, but decided to change this.

During SoCNoC (Southern Cross Novel Competition) in June 2010, I wrote and completed this story within the 30 days allowed. It came in roughly 55,000. I was so pleased with myself, and I loved this story so much.

In August, my laptop crashed, and I lost everything. Except for 26,000 words on Ice Planet (as it was known back then). This event, one of many events became the catalyst which lead me to the Doctors and diagnosed with Clinical Depression.

We tried natural remedies first, but they didn't work. It has taken three years to find the right medication for me, and six months of intensive counselling with a psychologist, to have the tools to move forward in life. For three years, my life was on hold. It's scary knowing that something is wrong, but unable to fix it. Your emotions are all wrong, you're constantly tired, and life just seems too hard.

I now have a life worth living, a life with supportive family and friends, those who have been with me and helped me to move forward, get me one foot in front of the other. From one step to a few steps. It was like learning to live again.

I still suffer from depression, and always will. It's a bit like alcoholism, once you have it; you can't "unhave" it.

It took me a while to come back to this story, but in 2013 I edited it, and brought it back to life, filling in the blanks. It doesn't seem to be as impressive as the first version, but I like this version. It is more real and more what I wanted for the story. Plus the romance is more of the focus of the story, rather than the subplot.

I always pictured Vyvica, standing with her hands on her hips, tapping her foot impatiently at me as I wrote the words. We would argue with each other, about what she would and wouldn't do, and when my editor called her Vyv, I could hear her saying "It's Vyv-ika."

Kelvaras, he was a tougher one to picture. He's a stirrer, and he wasn't really very clear to me until I started the rewrite. By then I had discovered Jason Stratham, and he reminded me so much of Kelvaras. Quiet, determined, but a stirrer none-the-less.

I've enjoyed working with the two of them, but pleased that I can finally put this one to bed, I can let them have their happy ever after.

Thank you for taking the time to read this book. If you enjoyed it, please consider leaving a review.

Gratitude and Beatitudes

Deryn Pitar- Critique Extraordinaire – I love the advice that you give, and your lovely comments.

Grace Lawler – New found critique partner and beta reader. Thanks for your insights.

Suzy Turner- for proofing my story and understanding that there are cultural differences.

Meryl Ferguson – an awesome proofreader, who pointed out some final little details to complete the story.

Leigh K Hunt – I love this girl. I fangirl over her all the time. Her cover art is just to die for. I tell her what I want and she exceeds my expectations. Check out her work at http://leighkhunt.com/dwell-design-press/

Melissa Pearl – my writing mentor - a wonderful friend and fellow writer who encourages me to follow my dreams

Tee Ayer – When times have been tough, we have been there for each other, spurring the other on. Thanks for being such an awesome person.

Cassie Hart- my ever busy editor. She provides interesting comments and commentary on my story, although I had to remind her a couple of times that she already knew the secret, and had to read the story as if she didn't. I love this girl! Just remember, "It's Vyv-ika."

To my son, Mum and Poppa – their loving encouragement makes it all worth- while.

Weblinks

Many of those who help me out have websites – check out their work

JC Hart – www.jchart.com
Hart and Stenhouse –
www.hartandstenhouse.wordpress.com

Melissa Pearl – www.melissapearl.come
T G Ayer – www.tgayer.com
Leigh K Hunt – www.leighkhunt.com
Virginnia De Parte - virginniadeparte.blogspot.co.nz/

If you enjoyed this book, feel free to leave a review at Goodreads, and whoever you purchased the book from.

Don't forget to sign up to my newsletter to get the inside knowledge on future new releases. You'll find it on the right hand sidebar on my website.

Stalk Catherine Mede on:
Facebook https://www.facebook.com/catherinemede
Pinterest http://www.pinterest.com/catherinemede/
Instagram
https://www.instagram.com/catherinemedenz
Twitter - @CatherineMedeNz
website - www.Catherinemede.com
email – Catherine@catherinemede.com

Who is Catherine Mede?

Catherine Mede lives in a rural village in the South Island of New Zealand with her son and two cats. When not writing, Catherine likes to read, draw and work in her garden and work.

Having developed a love for writing when she was at High School, it wasn't until she was in her thirties she decided to really get down and dirty with the words in her head.

Romance and Speculative Fiction are what Catherine likes to write because she understands the need to get lost in a love that sometimes seems mythical. And adding Fantasy elements just fulfils her needs to creative fanciful worlds.

When she was younger, she wrote to escape reality, now she writes it to allow others to enter a world where love has a happily ever after.

Cursed Love
Aotearoa Paranormal Romance

A family curse.

A lifetime of grieving.

Jinny Richards past and future are about to collide. Will she survive?

At 18, Virginia 'Jinny' Richards was a drug addict who fell in love with Dean Bradford. By 20, Dean was dead. Jinny believes the family curse is to blame, and never wants to fall in love again. She has worked hard to hide her past and now has a job as a successful Insurance Assessor.

Ethan Montgomery lost his wife to breast cancer. He's mourned her for three years and now he's ready to move on. He understands Jinny's pain, but he wants the feisty Jinny and nothing, not even a curse, will stand in his way.

When work throws them together, loving Ethan is the farthest thing from Jinny's mind. He's tardy and egotistical, even if he is good looking and makes her weak at the knees.

Things get further complicated when Steven Bradford turns out to be the client, bringing up the heartache and pain Jinny has carefully buried for eighteen years.

Will she find love a second time around? Or will the family curse claim another victim?

Coming Late 2016

Running Away
Aotearoa Contemporary Romance

Sometimes Life has a way of making you stop.

Larissa Green has had a rough run. She ditched her boyfriend, quit her job, and lost her flat all in a 24 hour period. She does what she does best. Larissa turns on her heels to escape by doing something totally out of character – going for a tramp.

Harley Orion is an English action movie star, in a toxic relationship. When his girlfriend accuses him of a serious offence, Harley freaks out and runs away to New Zealand until the storm blows over. Anonymity is assured when you stay at an isolated Lodge in the beautiful Abel Tasman National Park.

A fateful morning pushes the two together, and they can't deny the chemistry between them, but both are cautious. Harley has been stung by women, Larissa used by men. However they can't stop what happens between them.

Until the true nature of Harley's visit to New Zealand is revealed, destroying Larissa's hope of ending up with her dream man.

But life has a way of making things happen, when you least expect it.